CATCHING WATER IN A NET

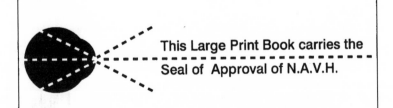

This Large Print Book carries the
Seal of Approval of N.A.V.H.

CATCHING
WATER
IN A NET

J. L. ABRAMO

Thorndike Press • Waterville, Maine

Published in 2002 by arrangement with St. Martin's Press, LLC.

Thorndike Press Large Print Americana Series.

The tree indicium is a trademark of Thorndike Press.

The text of this Large Print edition is unabridged.
Other aspects of the book may vary from the original edition.

Set in 16 pt. Plantin by Elena Picard.

Printed in the United States on permanent paper.

Library of Congress Cataloging-in-Publication Data

Abramo, J. L.
    Catching water in a net / J.L. Abramo.
        p. cm.
    ISBN 0-7862-3996-4 (lg. print : hc : alk. paper)
    1. Private investigators — California — San Francisco —
Fiction. 2. San Francisco (Calif.) — Fiction. 3. Organized
crime — Fiction. 4. Large type books. I. Title.
PS3601.B73 C3 2002
813'.6—dc21   2001058276

For my mother,
who didn't need to be an artist
to understand

ACKNOWLEDGMENTS

I would like to thank the Private Eye Writers of America and St. Martin's Press for offering the rare opportunity to novelists, and every year at that, to have their manuscripts read without the benefit of referrals or agents — for simply looking at the work.

I would like to thank those fellow writers, you know who you are, who (for no other reason than goodness of heart) helped me to feel, immediately, like a peer. And who generously shared their experiences with a middle-aged babe in the woods.

I would like to thank Raymond Chandler for admitting that *the perfect detective story cannot be written* — a valuable reminder to reader and writer alike.

I would like to thank the cities of Los Angeles and San Francisco for standing in for Paris and London in my tale. Any preferences expressed are purely subjective and not intended to unfairly exalt or deride either setting.

I would like to thank Jake Diamond for coming along at exactly the right time, with the hope that thanking a fictional character is not necessarily a mental-health danger sign.

I would like to thank Janis McWayne for being so sure.

DEAD
PIGEON

When it comes to private investigation,
nine times out of ten
the client is your worst enemy.

— JIMMY PIGEON

ONE

The phone on my desk rang so unexpectedly that I nearly spilled the Mylanta onto my only unstained necktie.

It was my trusty assistant calling from her sentry post out front.

Darlene Roman was different from most office receptionists in that the words *do you have an appointment* were not in her vocabulary.

Darlene greeted anyone who walked through our door as if it were our very first client, or might be our last.

"Yes, Darlene."

I tried not to slur the words, just in case Darlene was using the speakerphone.

"There's a woman here to see you."

I'd figured we had a guest. The place was small. Usually when Darlene wanted me she just hollered.

"Count to twenty, Darlene, and send her in," I said, determining that we were on a secure line.

11

"Is that one, two or one Mississippi, two Mississippi?"

I quickly assessed the condition of the desk.

"Make it one Montgomery, Alabama, two Montgomery, Alabama."

I tossed the bottle of Mylanta into the top drawer along with the plastic ashtray, remembering for a change to extinguish the burning cigarette. I opened a few dummy file folders and spread them across the desktop. No reason everyone had to know how slow business had been lately. I buried my face in the top folder, which incidentally held an unfriendly reminder from my ex-wife's attorney regarding past due alimony payments.

The date on the letter was from the last millennium.

The home of Diamond Investigation was a two-room affair above Molinari's Salumeria on Columbus Avenue. The leasing agent had described it as an Office Suite. The man was imaginative if nothing else.

Darlene's reception area was off the hallway entrance and my cubbyhole was directly behind hers, facing the street.

The elevator never worked, except as a homeless refuge occasionally.

The air, even at three stories above the avenue, always held a hint of provolone and Genoa salami.

"Mr. Diamond," my visitor said, walking through the door connecting the two small rooms.

Her voice could have broken glass. I felt a twinge in one of my molars. I slowly looked up from the folder, and the woman standing there could hardly be described in words. But I gave it a stab. She looked like a traced picture of herself.

She was plain as a cake doughnut.

"Can I help you, Miss . . . ?"

"Mrs. Mrs. Harding."

"Have a seat, Mrs. Harding."

"You can call me Evelyn."

"Sure, why not. Have a seat, Evelyn."

She looked down at the only other chair in the room and stood immobile. I jumped up and apologized as I moved the stack of folded boxer shorts from the offered seat. Darlene did a little laundry for me once in a while.

Evelyn sat tentatively and I returned to my own resting place, tossing the underwear into the bottom desk drawer, on top of my only clean shirt.

"So, Evelyn. How can I help you?"

"It's my husband."

If I had ten cents for every time I've heard that phrase I could have all three ties dry-cleaned.

"I can't find him," she added.

"I assure you, Mrs. Harding, he's not here."

"What?"

"It's a joke I use to relax new clients."

"It doesn't work."

"I can see that. How long has your husband been missing, Evelyn?"

"Since Saturday evening."

"That would be four days."

"I can see now why you came so highly recommended."

Evelyn Harding was as personable as an Office Depot catalog.

"Who did recommend me, Mrs. Harding?" I asked, turning the other cheek.

"Grace Shipley."

My response was not subtle. It resembled a knee jerk from the neck up. I pulled open the top desk drawer and took a long pull from the bottle of antacid. I had been so certain that I would never hear that name again, I couldn't be sure that I had actually heard it.

"Come again?"

"Grace Shipley."

It sounded pretty convincing the second time around.

"Could I ask you how you know Ms. Shipley?"

"Mr. Diamond, I came here to talk about my husband."

"Of course you did, Evelyn," I said. I think my voice may have cracked. "Have you thought about going to the police?"

"Finding my husband is already of interest to the Los Angeles Police Department, Mr. Diamond. I was hoping that you could help me locate him before they do."

"Call me Jake."

"Grace called you Jacob."

Grace had called me a lot of things.

"Why are the police interested in locating your husband?" I plowed on.

"They suspect that he killed his business partner."

"And why would they think that?"

"My husband's gun was found beside the body."

"Did he do it?"

"I don't believe so."

"But the murder weapon was found at the scene, and it belonged to your husband. Any theories about that?"

"My husband kept the gun in his office. The victim was killed in the office adjacent to his. The police have little else to go on."

"And?"

15

"They seem unwilling to grant that almost anyone could have taken the weapon and killed my husband's associate."

There you go; it could have been anyone. That should convince a jury.

"If your husband is innocent, why is he dodging the authorities?"

"I don't know. Perhaps he feels that no one will believe him; he's always lacked persuasive ability. That's why I need to find him. Before he gets himself hurt. Grace seems to think you can help."

Why me?

"Why me?" I asked. "There are plenty of very competent investigators in Los Angeles. I could highly recommend a good friend of mine down there. Jimmy Pigeon."

"I came to you, Mr. Diamond, because my husband's business partner was Jimmy Pigeon."

I managed to delay my reaction long enough to get the rough details from Evelyn Harding and then quickly sent her on her way, assuring her that I would stay in touch.

She was barely through the door before the surprise and shock that came with the news of Jimmy Pigeon's death hit me like a sucker punch.

I opened the top desk drawer and pulled out the ashtray and the bottle.

This time it was the bottle of bourbon.

16

Two

After a few shots and a smoke I pulled myself together. At least enough to give what I had heard some attention.

I went over the facts as Evelyn Harding had laid them out.

The toughest fact being that I hadn't heard about any of it before.

Evelyn's husband, Harry Harding, was a co-founder of Ex-Con.com. An Internet company that located felons released from prison. There appeared to be a potential clientele for that sort of information among those seeking retribution and those fearing it, from victims and families of victims on one hand to arresting officers, prosecutors, and jurists on the other.

The co-co-founder was Jimmy Pigeon.

The late Jimmy Pigeon.

Shot to death with a gun belonging to Harry Harding.

It was Jimmy who got me started in the

business of private investigation.

For a moment I wondered why Jimmy hadn't brought me on board the dot com enterprise. In fact, he'd never mentioned it. I liked to think that Jimmy considered me a worthy collaborator.

On second thought I figured that what Jimmy Pigeon needed was a financial backer, not another penniless gumshoe. Locating ex-cons would have been right up Jimmy's alley. Harding must have been the moneyman.

I finally realized that I was playing cat and mouse with the question that was really bothering me: If Jimmy was in danger or in some kind of trouble, why hadn't he come to me for help?

Now Jimmy Pigeon was dead and Harry Harding was hiding from everyone, including his wife.

In Harry Harding's favor was the fact that there were more than a few unsavory characters who would not be brokenhearted over Jimmy's death. Jimmy Pigeon was good at his work, the kind of work that tended to create enemies.

But Harding's gun and his disappearance were top-notch credentials for a bona fide murder suspect.

Unfortunately, I could think of no better

way to get started than to pay a visit to Vinnie Stradivarius. When it came to Jimmy Pigeon, no one knew better than Vinnie. Vinnie was like a son to Jimmy, like the son Jimmy never had.

Albeit the kind of son that would put any father to task.

Vinnie was a handful, constantly getting into jams that took more than a little effort and creativity to pry the kid out of. For reasons of his own, which I could have been too selfish to understand, Jimmy had taken on the challenge.

Part of Jimmy's strategy was to try keeping Vinnie busy. To that end Jimmy often had Vinnie assist in his investigations, just enough to make the kid feel that he was being useful, nothing that would totally blow a case. It gave Vinnie less time to get into mischief and gave Jimmy an excuse to throw the kid some rent money.

I wondered who in the world was going to take on the thankless chore of watching out for Vinnie Stradivarius now that Jimmy was gone. I shuddered at the thought, so I immediately abandoned it.

You are going to hear many different opinions about the type of person who chooses private investigation as a vocation. Believe all of them.

Every PI will give you his or her rationale. Often without being asked.

Here's mine.

Jimmy Pigeon.

I had never met anyone quite like Jimmy. His walk, his talk, his self-confidence, and, above all, his honesty.

In Jimmy Pigeon I finally saw what I wanted to be when I grew up. I'm reluctant to admit that I was nearly thirty-five when it happened. And that I'm still working on it.

Nine to five was never in the cards for me. I had always imagined that movie actors had the ideal career. I tried it for a while myself but kept being cast as a thug. And a supporting thug at that.

It was on a movie set, in fact, that I first met Jimmy Pigeon. He was there as technical adviser for a B thriller in which an over-the-hill PI, played by an over-the-hill actor who I won't name, was searching for a senator's daughter held ransom by a group of thugs, one of whom looked a lot like me. Pigeon and I became fast friends and he inspired me to turn in my SAG card for an investigator's license. I was at a point in my acting career where every suggestion sounded perfect. I left Hollywood for a desk in Jimmy's Santa Monica office and learned the ropes. Once I had been given enough rope to hang myself I decided to head north to San Francisco to set up shop on my own.

The move had two major advantages. It was four hundred miles farther from Los Angeles and four hundred miles closer to Mom's cooking.

I also had Jimmy Pigeon to thank for the first client who walked into my small office above the Italian deli in North Beach. Sally French hired me to find her biological mother. Jimmy, who knew her adoptive father from his college days at Santa Barbara, had given Sally my name. I was able to locate her mother, who became my mother-in-law, though not for very long. I couldn't blame Jimmy. He meant well.

Now Evelyn Harding had hired me to find her husband, apparently in the hope that I could help establish that he wasn't responsible for Jimmy Pigeon's murder.

Was anyone really interested in finding out who did kill Jimmy?

I was.

I owed Jimmy that much.

I took one more hit of bourbon and went looking for Vinnie Stradivarius.

THREE

Vinnie Stradivarius was known as Vinnie Strings by friend and foe alike, though not many made the connection. Vinnie was tall and as thin as a rail, with a dark complexion and a mop of red hair that made him look more like a lit cigar than a violin. Vinnie had a favorite saying.

"You know," he would tell me or anyone who would listen, "I was born at exactly the right time in exactly the right place."

That was before he went to New York City on an errand for Jimmy Pigeon and passed an Off-Track Betting parlor.

Vinnie Strings was fickle.

"And these OTB joints are on every other corner, Jake; you wouldn't believe it. It's just my rotten luck that I wasn't born in Brooklyn."

It took a leap of faith to believe almost anything that Vinnie had to say. And when he was being factual, Vinnie rarely had anything to tell you that you didn't already know. But listening to him carry on was sometimes amusing. In very small doses.

I was hoping that Strings could surprise me with something that I didn't know about for a change. Something about what Jimmy had been up to.

Vinnie ran between San Francisco and Los Angeles helping Jimmy out with odd errands, most of which were hardly necessary. Vinnie had an apartment on Haight and Parker, a block off the park. When Strings was down in LA he crashed at Jimmy's place. Jimmy Pigeon always found Vinnie most helpful when the kid was up here.

Vinnie's apartment was like something out of a Godard film, which wasn't all that surprising since *Breathless* was his favorite flick. In place of a poster of Bogart, Strings had mounted a two-by-three-foot black-and-white of Belmondo on his living room wall. As you came into the room you felt as if you had just walked into a scene on television, some time before the advent of color TV. Strings had ashtrays scattered everywhere, which he never emptied, though he didn't smoke himself.

Vinnie was the only person I had ever met who didn't have a kitchen table.

When Vinnie wasn't doing legwork for

Jimmy Pigeon I could usually count on finding him at one of the local racetracks or at the Northern California answer to OTB. The place was situated in the basement of a house in the Mission District equipped with a satellite dish and three big-screen TVs. It was called the Finnish Line after its owners, two tall blond brothers from Finland. Since I knew that Strings wasn't doing any work for Jimmy anymore, ever, and I didn't want to spend all day running from one pony track to another, I headed for the Mission.

As I drove I was feeling bad about not keeping in closer touch with Jimmy Pigeon, about having to hear about his death from a stranger.

Granted, I avoided Los Angeles at every opportunity, but I could have used the telephone more often.

Being very proficient at rationalization, I would tell myself that the phone lines went both ways.

On top of that, feeling bad wouldn't get me anywhere.

The baboon at the door must have recognized me, because he let me in without the song and dance. Vinnie Strings was sitting in front of one of the giant TV screens with a fistful of twenties, yelling something about a glue factory. When he saw me he rushed over.

"Jesus, Jake, did you hear what happened to Jimmy?"

"An hour ago. Evelyn Harding dropped by my office."

"Harding. I always had a bad feeling about that guy."

It seemed as if Vinnie was a lot more informed than I was.

It was a demoralizing thought.

"You think Harding killed Jimmy?" I asked.

"It looks that way; trouble is, it's too obvious."

"Oh?"

"Harding figures to make a bundle with Jimmy out of the way."

"How so?"

"They got an offer for their business," Vinnie said, "a million bucks."

"How come nobody told me about the business, Vinnie?"

"I thought you knew about the Internet gig, Jake. I just figured you weren't talking about it because you were sore that Jimmy hadn't cut you in."

"And why did I have to hear about Jimmy's death from Evelyn Harding?"

"Honest, Jake, I only heard about it two nights ago myself. I'd been trying to reach Jimmy for days. Two homicide dicks barged into my place. They broke the news to me like it was somebody's cat died. I thought I was going to pass out. On top of that they start asking questions like I was a suspect or something. I was a wreck. I am a wreck."

"Calm down, Vinnie," I said.

It was beginning to dawn on Strings that Jimmy's condition was final.

I thought it would be better to keep Vinnie talking. Then I realized that he needed no help in that department; he was running on as if the coin were about to drop.

"And when the cops left, they gave me a message from Ray Boyle: 'Don't say anything to anyone, especially Jake Diamond,' like it's a warning. Boyle will break the news to Diamond himself, they tell me."

Ray Boyle was a homicide detective down in LA.

Ray Boyle and I went back some.

I could understand why Ray may have preferred to hold off notifying me, at least until he had a suspect in custody. Boyle would want to keep me out of his hair.

But it wasn't like Vinnie to consider Boyle's preferences.

"Since when are you dancing to Boyle's tune, Vinnie?"

"Boyle kept me out of some trouble the last time I was down that way, and he's holding it over my head. Believe me, Jake, I wanted to tell you right away. I've been going nuts trying to stay away from the telephone, and trying to convince myself that Boyle would call you or that it was just a bad dream."

I bought it. It was the only item on the shelf.

"Who was offering the million?" I asked.

"Fat cat down in LA. Walter Richman."

Disaster flicks came to mind.

"The movie producer?"

"Movies, TV, telecommunications. Big on acquisition," Vinnie said.

"So, Jimmy checked out just when his ship came in."

"Yeah, but the thing is, Jimmy didn't want to sell. Harding was game; to him I guess it was a quick score. Invest a hundred grand, take a five hundred percent profit in six months, and get out."

"But Jimmy?"

"For Jimmy it was different. The thing was his baby, his brainchild, and he wasn't ready to give it up. He liked watching it crawl. He had more invested in it than money."

"So what now? Who's minding the store?"

"It just sort of runs itself. There's an office down on Wilshire, a manager, a bunch

27

of college kids at computers, services billed on credit cards. With Harding missing in action, I suppose that his old lady is in charge."

If Vinnie didn't come up for air soon, he was going to need a decompression chamber.

"How about Jimmy's end?"

"I don't know. I mean, who did he have?" said Vinnie. "Maybe he left a will or something."

"When was the last time you saw Jimmy?"

"I was down there last week," Vinnie said. "I saw Jimmy just four days before he was killed. Jimmy and Harry Harding were going at it over the buyout offer. I thought Jimmy was going to tear Harding's lungs out."

"If Jimmy had made some arrangements, who would know about it?"

"There's a lawyer down there he traded services with. What was his name? You know the guy, I think. Bald dude with a ponytail. Looks fucking ridiculous."

"Spencer?" I asked, afraid of the answer.

"Yeah, that's the guy. Dick Spencer. You know him?"

"Yeah, I know him."

I neglected to mention that Dick Spencer did a little trading of services with my ex-wife as well.

"Maybe he knows something about Jimmy's estate. It's the only lead I can think of. You heading down there?"

"Guess I will."

"Want company?"

"No thanks."

"I'm sick about what happened to Jimmy. I'll do anything to help."

I wasn't quite ready for Vinnie's kind of help.

"Any idea where Harding might have skipped off to?" I asked, trying to sidestep the issue.

"None. His wife want to find him?"

"So she says. And before the cops do."

"I'll keep my ears open. But if the LAPD is gunning for him he most likely headed south. Way south."

"Think Harding could go ahead and sell the business to Richman?"

"Good question. You might ask Spencer when you see him."

"OK. Check in with Darlene while I'm gone if you can," I said, hoping to put the idea of following me down to LA further from Vinnie's mind. "If something comes up that you think you can handle, cover for me."

I was biting my tongue as I said it.

And I was going to catch hell from Darlene for passing Vinnie off on her.

"Sure thing, *compadre*."

"If Jimmy did leave a will, what do you think the chances are he named you in it, Strings?"

"About the same as the chances that he named you, Jake."

"Sorry."

"No problem."

"How'd you do on the NBA Championship?"

"Massacred. Planning to drop in on your client while you're down there, Jake?"

"I might. Why do you ask?"

"Just thought you'd want to know that Grace Shipley might be staying with her."

"You're right. I would want to know that. What's their connection?"

"Old school chums, I guess. When Pigeon was looking for start-up capital, Grace put him together with Harding. The Hardings have a daughter who just got out of high school. Jimmy mentioned that Grace was in for the graduation and she was staying with the Hardings in Beverly Hills."

"I didn't realize that Jimmy and Grace kept in touch."

Something else that Jimmy had never told me about.

Jimmy may have guessed that I'd be better off not knowing.

Maybe that was why Jimmy had neglected to mention his new business venture as well.

"You know Grace," said Vinnie. "She always seemed to need a helping hand. And you know how much Jimmy liked to lend a helping hand."

One of Jimmy's helping hands had been reserved almost entirely for Vinnie Strings. I had to resist the strong temptation to feel sorry for the kid.

And wonder when the next big jolt over Jimmy's death was going to hit me.

If I got all wrapped up in that now, we'd both be falling without parachutes.

"When are you heading down to LA?" Vinnie asked.

"As soon as possible. Probably tonight."

"I know where you can get cheap plane tickets."

"Thanks, but I think I'll take the Impala. I can use the drive to prepare myself."

"For Grace?"

"For Dick Spencer. For talking my way out of two grand or so in back alimony. Who do you have in the next race?" I asked as I headed out.

"The way my luck is going, Worthless Nag."

FOUR

My most cherished possession, aside from my hoe-sharp wit and my two-dollar smile, is unarguably the 1963 Chevrolet Impala convertible in Joey Russo's garage.

Red exterior, black leather interior, straight six, three on the column.

I'd known Joey for almost five years; he was my second client after Sally French. I'm guessing that Jimmy sent him my way also, but Joey never said. Joey was looking for a guy who owed him money. A lot of money. I took Russo's word that there would be no breaking of limbs and accepted the case. When I found the guy, he was so terrified of Joey that he forked over what he owed Russo plus a C-note to help me forget where I'd found him. Joey seemed satisfied; I made the extra hundred and earned a safe haven for the Chevy in the bargain. Joey told me that he didn't want financial compensation, while I insisted that I pay rent for the prime garage space. After a

round of quibbling he accepted fifty a mont
which was quite a bargain.

The garage was behind the Russo hou
on Sixth Avenue, between Clement and t
park, up the street from the Green App
Bookstore. When I wanted to use the Ir
pala I drove over in my everyday vehicle
1978 Toyota Corona four-door sedan wi
210,000 miles on the odometer and a ho
in the floorboard, and left it parked on t
street outside of Joey's place. Parking spac
are literally impossible to find in the city. I
said that the only way to get a parking spa
in San Francisco is to buy a parked car. Jo
always managed to have a spot waiting
front of his house when I came to get t
Chevy. I don't know how. I never asked.

I parked the Toyota and walked down
the bookstore, thinking that I could u
something to read for the trip. The colle
kid who swooped down on me when
walked through the door tried very hard
be helpful. She suggested the new priv
eye novel by Sue Gideon. I passed.

The last time I had read a book by
woman author I hated all men for a mon
including myself.

I opted for a dog-eared copy of *A Tal
Two Cities* instead.

Dickens in hand, I walked back to the

rage, pulled the Chevy out of the driveway, and started toward LA. I figured I'd make it down to San Luis Obispo in time for a late dinner and then grab a motel room for the night. Read a bit about the best of times and the worst of times and hit the sack. The plan was to rise early and pay a visit to Sam Chambers at the Men's Colony before continuing to Los Angeles.

I headed out Geary to Van Ness and 101 South.

As I drove I realized that I was looking forward to seeing Sam. It had been some time since I'd dropped in to visit him at the prison. At the same time, I wasn't too excited about having to drop in on Dick Spencer. And boy, would old Dick be surprised by a visit from the guy who'd been avoiding his phone calls two or three times a month for the past four months or so.

Ok, I know what you're thinking. Diamond the deadbeat. Denying his ex-wife the alimony she has coming to her. Give me a break.

When Sally French walked into my office five years ago and became my first client she was working in the Lingerie Department at May's. Her employee discounts were a big part of her appeal. When I located her birth mother, Sally suddenly became heir to a substantial fortune. She was so grateful she agreed to marry me. The bottom line is that Sally needs $500 a month from me the way she needs another pair of babydolls.

I made good time down to Obispo, getting in just before nine in the evening.

I sat down to a plate of cheese enchiladas and a couple of Coronas at a Tex-Mex joint off the highway and then checked into the Quality Inn.

What a misnomer.

The desk clerk asked if I wanted nonsmoking or smoking. I told her smoking would be just the thing.

I took a cold shower, not really by choice, and settled in with the novel. At page 52 the description of Lucie Manette was conjuring up images of Grace Shipley and I had to put the book down. I couldn't blame Dickens. Checking the baseball standings might have had the same effect.

I called down to the desk clerk to request a 7:00 a.m. wake-up call and hung up when I was fairly certain that she knew what I was driving at. I smoked one more Camel straight to take full advantage of the special accommodations, which mysteriously lacked a single ashtray, turned off the light, and tried to get some rest.

I dreamed that Lucie Manette was telling me to take a hike.

FIVE

The telephone beside the bed woke me at precisely 7:00 a.m. Life is full of little surprises. I picked up the receiver, said, "Thank you," and quickly hung up. It was too early for light repartee. I was really in no mood to hear someone tell me to have a nice day. I had other plans.

I jumped into the shower hoping for an improvement over the night before. Lucky me. The water temperature had skyrocketed to lukewarm.

I wished I had something to bring to Sam. Then again, anything he could really use wasn't allowed in.

I checked my pockets to be sure I didn't walk away with the room key and then remembered that the thing that opened the door was the little plastic card that I had used in lieu of an ashtray.

Sam Chambers was called Sam the Sham by his very closest friends, or by reckless imbeciles. I counted myself among the chosen few who could address him as the Sham without getting my teeth knocked out. The chosen few had become fewer with the death of Jimmy Pigeon.

I'd met Sam while working on the set of a movie. My last movie. The same B movie set where I had met Jimmy Pigeon, who was there to teach a has-been bargain matinee idol how to act hard-boiled. Sam Chambers was cast as one of my co-thugs.

As often as I had played the thug, the role was less a stretch for Sam. Casting Sam as a petty criminal was like casting Walter Brennan as a crusty old-timer. Don't get me wrong; I liked Sam. And Sam never hurt a soul who didn't need hurting.

There was a scene in the movie where the thugs are debating what to do with the senator's daughter once the ransom had been paid. The young girl playing the kidnap victim wasn't a very accomplished actress, but after all, this wasn't *Schindler's List*.

The director commented on the kid's acting ability by suggesting we cut her up into little pieces and put us all out of our misery.

Sweet guy.

The girl began crying and Sam was attempting to calm her down while at the same time shouting at the director to apologize to the poor kid.

The director said he didn't need advice from some lowlife named Sam the Sham and Sam walked over and floored him. To say that Sam was short-tempered would be like saying that Judy Garland could sing.

In the end the director apologized to the kid after spitting out a few teeth and the cameras began rolling again. For the rest of the shoot he chose to direct Sam by hardly looking in his direction.

That was Sam's last movie role also, and Jimmy Pigeon took us both under his wing. I went to work for Jimmy, but Sam returned to his day job. Now he was serving three to five for armed robbery.

Jimmy and I went to bat for Sam when he came up on trial for the rap. We dug up evidence that we were confident would prove that Sam was just trying to get back what he had coming. Unfortunately, the disagreement was over his split from an earlier robbery, so our argument that the guy Sam tried to take off actually owed him the bread didn't carry a lot of weight.

To make things worse, the presiding judge had had a previous run-in with Sam. The last time Sam had stood before him, Sam called the judge a pachydermatous fascist.

Tough luck for Sam, since elephants and fascists never forget.

I decided to grab a quick breakfast before heading over to the prison. I hadn't been out there for a while but doubted they had put in an espresso bar yet. Though it wasn't out of the question. I thought I could maybe sneak a jelly doughnut in to Sam, if I could find one that was too small to conceal a file.

The eggs were cold, the potatoes were raw, the toast was burned, and the waitress was rude. I left her a buck, reminding her that it was good for twenty minutes' long distance. The joint was fresh out of tiny jelly doughnuts.

I put down the top of the Chevy and headed out to the Men's Colony. As I drove, I wondered if Sam Chambers had heard the news about Jimmy before I had. It wouldn't surprise me; Sam and Jimmy had more mutual acquaintances. I had distanced myself from the old LA circle.

I may have suggested earlier that I was the only person who really cared about Jimmy's fate. That's not entirely true. Sam would care. And come to think of it, I'm sure that Vinnie Strings cared also. Not an all-star cast of mourners, I'll admit, but better than being missed by no one, I suppose.

In any case, I hated to be the one to break

it to Sam if he didn't know of Jimmy's demise. An hour later I learned that Sam thought he knew a great deal about it.

The guard who patted me down at the prison check-in might have had a future as a French masseuse. Finding nothing more dangerous on my person than my American Express Gold Card, dangerous to no one but myself, he escorted me into an ugly gray room. There I would wait twenty-five minutes for Sam Chambers to appear on the other side of a glass partition so I could talk with him through an ancient handset.

If I had thought to smuggle in a spray bottle of Windex, I could have passed the time a lot more constructively.

When Sam took the seat opposite mine, a half-inch of glass and three years minus possible time off for good behavior between us, he didn't look too good.

We picked up our respective heavy black phone receivers. It wasn't difficult to determine which one of them had been smashed against the window most often.

"Good to see you, Sam," I said.

"Thanks for coming, Jake," he said.

Because I was feeling derelict about not visiting more often I listened carefully for any hint of accusation in his voice. As paranoid as I tend to be at times, especially when inside prison walls, I concluded that Sam's greeting was sincere.

"You don't look well, Sam," I said.

Never accuse me of being tactful.

"I could say it was just the food," said Sam, "but I would be understating the problem."

Sometimes it's smart to simply not ask, so I didn't.

"I've got some bad news," I said. Might as well throw in a pinch of salt.

"Before you go on, I have a headline that may interest you."

"What's that?"

"I think I know who killed Jimmy Pigeon," he said.

"Oh?" I said.

"Does the name Bobo Bigelow ring a bell?"

It sounded vaguely familiar. Visiting time at the prison was too short for guessing games, so I threw in the towel.

"Refresh my memory."

"The cat who was supplying Benzes and Beemers to the Saudi consulate in LA. Same cars that were disappearing from driveways in Beverly Hills and Marina del Ray."

"Oh, that Bobo Bigelow. The guy with a noggin like Mr. Potato Head."

"Yeah, that's the guy."

"What about him?"

"Well," said Sam, "after he did four years at Chino for Grand Theft Auto he came out and changed his name, didn't want anyone whose car he had reallocated looking him up to give him grief."

How did Sam know all this stuff?

"What's he calling himself?" I asked.

"Spuds Lonegan. So Bigelow gets this new gig going. Something with airline vouchers. I couldn't really understand how it works, but he was making very big bucks. Suddenly Bigelow's up on charges again for fraud. Interstate transportation, something, a federal rap. Some plastic surgeon from the Valley dropped a dime on him."

"Sam, how do you hear all this stuff?" I had to ask.

"A kid named Lefty Wright just got sent up here from LA. Cops caught him with a pocket full of jewelry inside the house of some movie actress; can't remember her name. Lefty filled us in at dinner last night."

"What's all this got to do with Jimmy?"

"Jimmy tracked Bobo down for the sawbones, through his Web company."

"So you think that Bobo, or Spuds whatever, snuffed Jimmy for blowing his alias? Is that a hunch, Sam? I mean, do you have anything a little more bankable to go on?"

"Bigelow got busted and Jimmy got iced the very next day."

Not exactly as persuasive as a DNA match.

"You may have something there, Sam. I'll check it out."

Sam had been right about understating the problem. It was definitely more than just the food.

I spent the remainder of our visit listening to Sam talk about what prison inmates talk about: getting out. I told him, as I had times before, that he was welcome up in San Francisco as soon as he was released and that I would have work for him. I was sure that Jimmy Pigeon had offered Sam the same down in LA. I was also sure that he would most likely go back to burglary. It was what he knew and loved best.

I left Sam Chambers with a less than convincing promise that I'd get back to see him soon.

As I continued south I tried the obligatory benefit of the doubt on for size, but Sam's theory involving Bobo Bigelow didn't wash.

Bigelow would more likely go after the sore loser who fingered him.

Jimmy held no malice for Bobo, and Bigelow knew that. For Jimmy it was just business, and Bobo could appreciate that, too. It appeared as if Sam was trying to utilize a human attribute that he was sadly a little shy of these days. Imagination. It made me somewhat melancholy.

But hey, who am I, Copernicus? If I had all the angles figured out, I wouldn't be going to speak with a toad like Dick Spencer. If nothing else panned out, I'd keep Bobo Bigelow in mind.

I'd made a phone call to Willie Dogtail at my last gas-up. Willie was an old crony from those bygone days in Santa Monica when I was enrolled at the Jimmy Pigeon institute of investigation and surveillance. Dogtail, a full-blooded Sioux with family ties going back to Crazy Horse, had a small house on the beach with a spare room for a visiting paleface from the north. And Willie always kept an ear to the sand. I thought he might know something about Jimmy's final days.

I stopped for a bite outside of Ventura, since I hadn't touched my breakfast.

I thought about calling Evelyn Harding to tell her I was on my way. I let the impulse pass, deciding that it could wait until I was settled in at Willie's place.

As I continued south on Route 101 and down through Thousand Oaks I was reminded how lucky I was to have escaped

44

Southern California. When I took the turnoff onto Route 27 at Woodland Hills toward the Pacific Coast Highway I could begin to make out the dark cloud that permanently hovered over Los Angeles and could swear I felt the city already doing a number on my respiratory system.

When I reached the beach, the house was empty. I knew where Willie hid the key, so I let myself in. There was a note from Dogtail on the kitchen table, under an unopened fifth of George Dickel Sour Mash, saying that if I didn't make myself at home he'd break my thumbs when he got back.

A welcome to warm the heart of any weary traveler.

I thought again about calling Evelyn Harding but was still afraid that Grace might answer the telephone.

So I had a happy reunion with Mr. Dickel instead.

The bourbon must have lulled me to sleep. I guess the trip had worn me out more than I knew.

The next thing I remember was being woken by a faint *rat-a-tat* and opening my eyes to find Willie Dogtail drumming on my shoulder with a pair of sesame-seeded bread sticks.

"I brought lasagna back for you and

George D., Kemosabe. You can sleep when you're dead."

I thought I was looking up into the face of a giant insect. Willie was wearing a pair of sunglasses with bubble lenses that made him look a lot like David Hedison after swapping body parts with the fly.

"What time is it?" I asked.

"Time to stash the bedroll, pardner; we got some catching up to do on this here cattle drive."

Willie Dogtail had rustic-speak down pat.

"Have any coffee?" I asked.

"Sure do, Wyatt. Chicory?"

I should have known better.

"No thanks."

He walked over to the stove, put nearly a quarter-can of Folgers into a medium saucepan, filled whatever space was left with water, and placed it on the front burner. Then he lit the burner and cranked the gas flame to 10.

"We'll give it about five minutes; how the hell are you?"

I could feel the hair on my chest rearranging itself to make room for the new arrivals.

"I'm good, Willie. That lasagna have any meat in it?"

"No way. No dairy, either. Want me to heat it up for you?"

46

"No thanks, just a fork, a straw, whatever." No dairy?

"Guess you heard what happened to Jimmy Pigeon," he said, handing me a ceramic soupspoon with STOLEN FROM TOMMY WONG's MANDARIN BUFFET inscribed on the bottom.

"Yeah, that's the reason I came down. Know much about it?"

"Well, nothing definite, but I have some ideas."

Who didn't? Ah, what the hell.

"Run it by me."

"Hold on; that coffee's starting to boil. You're gonna love the mud, Tex."

I must have also been hungrier than I knew, because I inhaled the tofu lasagna. But it was Dogtail's camp coffee, not the pasta, that was sticking to my ribs. If this was his way of keeping me awake and chatty, he had it covered for a good week and a half.

Thing was, he did most of the talking. Willie's theories about who pulled the plug on Jimmy Pigeon were as grounded in fact as Sam the Sham's, only more elaborate.

I tried listening to the best of my ability, but most of the time I could hardly hear his voice over the buzzing in my ears from the caffeine.

It was going to be a long night.

Dogtail's first hypothesis about what may

47

have done Jimmy in revolved around the single most dangerous animal in the world: a jealous husband with a Latin-rooted surname.

According to Willie, Jimmy was making time with a saucy number named Tina Bella. At least that's what she called herself when Jimmy and I first met her in a Malibu nightclub six years before. Tina was singing in the club, wasn't bad at it, either, and she and Jimmy hit it off immediately. Jimmy and Tina's thing had always been an on-again, off-again arrangement, and for the most part they managed to stay out of trouble. Then about a year ago Tina Bella became Mrs. Alfonzo Pazzo. When Jimmy and I talked about that little development we both wisely agreed that on again, off again had best be off for good.

"Do you know what *pazzo* means in Italian?" Dogtail asked.

"I give up."

"Insane."

"Is that why they call him Crazy Al?"

"Not really. He'd be Crazy Al if his name were Jones. Al Pazzo is one maladjusted white man."

"And Jimmy was seeing Tina again after she married Pazzo?"

"That's the tale."

"Crazy Al finds out and kills Jimmy?"

"It's a thought," said Willie, "but I have an alternative scenario."

So much for trying to narrow down the list of suspects.

"Let's hear it," I sighed.

Willie's second supposition made the first resemble the Gospel truth.

"There's word going around that Vinnie Strings might be involved."

"Around from where?" I growled, surprised by my anger.

"The name Spuds Lonegan mean anything to you?"

"Bobo Bigelow?"

"That's the one."

"And this habitual con artist is putting the word out that Vinnie had something to do with Jimmy's murder?" I said, trying to control my anger.

"Talking up a storm."

"That's bullshit!" I yelled, throwing Tommy Wong's spoon against the wall.

"Don't shoot the messenger, Ringo. I'm just relating what I heard."

It was impossible. Jimmy Pigeon had been a little like a father to Vinnie Strings and a lot like a guardian angel. How could Vinnie possibly profit from Jimmy's death? And why was a lowlife like Bobo Bigelow pointing fingers?

"Got any Mylanta?"

"There's a roll of Tums in the medicine cabinet. Sit tight."

"That's OK, Willie. I'll get it," I said, and headed for the john.

I chewed four or five tablets and sat on the toilet seat wondering what the hell I had gotten myself into. There was a guy I grew up with went to pick up his automobile from the service garage one day. He couldn't find anyone to go with him, so he borrowed a car and drove over himself. When he got there he realized that he had two vehicles on his hands. So what he did was drive the first car about a quarter-mile, get out, run back to the garage and pick up the second car, drive that one about a quarter-mile past the first, run back to the first car, drive it about a quarter-mile past the second, and so on until he finally got both cars where they needed to be. I had thought that was the most idiotic and counterproductive activity I could ever imagine until now, when I took a close look at how I was handling the investigation into the murder of Jimmy Pigeon.

"You OK in there, Sundance?" Willie called from outside the bathroom door.

Sure.

Just great.

SIX

I woke the next morning with a pounding headache compliments of George Dickel, one of the few names not implicated in the shooting of Jimmy Pigeon. I thought briefly about the "have another drink" remedy but wisely decided to go the food route instead.

I thanked Willie for his hospitality, if not for his insights, and headed out the Santa Monica Freeway toward Los Angeles. I hopped off at Culver City for a bite to eat and a half-gallon of orange juice to wash it down.

I sat at a booth in a Denny's Restaurant staring at a plate of blueberry pancakes as I chewed four Excedrin. After Dogtail's recipe the night before, Denny's brew tasted like what it was. Coffee-flavored water.

I decided that I had better get straight to Dick Spencer and try to avoid any more monumental revelations that put me off the track. Unfortunately, it wasn't in the cards.

51

When I saw the shadow sliding into the bench seat opposite mine I absolutely did not want to look up to see who had joined me. Since the blueberries were winning the stare-down contest I had no choice.

Aside from the ears, which were slightly larger, and the nose, which was more like a radish than a carrot tip, the resemblance to Mr. Potato Head was uncanny.

"You don't look too good, Diamond."

Everyone's a critic.

"Good morning, Bobo. Or should I call you Spuds?"

"I heard you're looking to find out who killed your buddy Jimmy Pigeon."

"As a matter of fact, your name came up."

"You know better."

I thought I did.

"So why are you turning the spotlight on Vinnie Stradivarius?"

"I heard some things through the grapevine."

Knowing something about the crowd that Bigelow ran in, I figured it for a sour grapevine.

"How'd you find me?"

"I was coming to see you at Dogtail's place and arrived just as you were pulling away. I thought you had better taste in coffee."

"I did until last night. I'm not too keen on hearing Vinnie's name thrown around haphazardly. Would you mind telling me what juicehead on your so-called grapevine sold you on such a flaky idea?"

"Do you know an ambulance chaser name of Dick Spencer?" Bobo asked.

Oh boy.

"Is he your lawyer, too?"

"Yeah. I'm up on a rap for hawking airline ticket vouchers. It's a really beautiful scam. I could tell you how it works."

"No thanks. Who referred you to Spencer?"

"After I got busted I went to talk with Pigeon about how he might want to consider being a little more selective in his choice of Web clients. That was the day before Pigeon bought it, but we parted with an understanding and Jimmy suggested I look up Spencer. Whoever thinks I had anything to do with throwing Jimmy's switch belongs in a cell up in the Men's Colony."

I could have told Bobo that it was already done, but I resisted.

"So, in summation, what you're telling me is that Dick Spencer told you that Vinnie was somehow tied in to Jimmy's death?"

"Not exactly."

"C'mon, Bigelow. My pancakes are getting ice-cold."

"Spencer just sort of mentioned in passing that Strings is about to come into an inheritance and I made the leap."

"Nice leap, Evel. While you're at it maybe you can tell me where Jimmy Hoffa strayed off to." I forgot to ask about Cock Robin.

"All right, I admit I was out of line. My name was making the rounds and I felt like kicking back. So I headed over this morning when I heard you were at Willie Dogtail's place, to try to square it with you. I really have no idea who took Jimmy out. I just wanted to make sure that you didn't think it was me."

Bigelow was taking circular reasoning to new levels of perfection.

"How did you know I was at Dogtail's to begin with?"

"Willie called me, said he got a little drunk last night, and may have mentioned my name to you in vain," said Bigelow. "I'd been getting Dogtail cheap flights down to Acapulco; he must have been afraid I'd cut him off if I heard it from someone else."

"Do everyone a favor, Bigelow, and put a sock in it. Stick to talking about what you know, regardless of how much it limits your conversation."

"Fair enough, Diamond. And just to show you that I'm serious about taking your advice to heart, the next time I tell you something that I'm sure you'll be eager to hear, it will be one hundred percent verifiable."

"And when will that be?" I asked, even though his radish nose was flashing at me like a red traffic light.

"I know where you can find Harry Harding," he said.

Bobo Bigelow pushed over a paper napkin on which he had written the Alvarado Street address where he claimed Harding could be found.

It's my nature to lean toward skepticism, so I didn't exactly snatch it up off the table and jump for joy.

"How is it you happen to have this breaking news?" I asked.

"Harry called me for a plane ticket; he's looking for a flight to anywhere that's at least as far south as Brazil. I told him to give me a day and I'd drop by with something."

"Anyone else know about this?"

"Just you and me."

"Keep it that way."

"Want some company?" he asked.

"No, but thanks for asking," I said, making every effort in the inflection of each word to unmask my sarcasm.

"Don't you think you owe me a little something for the tip?" Bobo asked.

I pushed the plate of cold pancakes over to his side of the table and got up to leave.

If I didn't get to eat something soon I was going to be in bad trouble.

"Diamond!" he called as I headed for the door.

"What is it, Spuds?" I said, not turning to look back.

"Let me know if you ever need a great deal on airfare."

I paid the cashier at the door, climbed into the Chevy, and started back on the freeway to Los Angeles.

I tried unsuccessfully to con myself into thinking that I was making progress.

I glanced down at the paper napkin on the seat beside me. If it sounds too good to be true it probably is.

Or as Jimmy Pigeon might have put it: *When you follow up a lead from a guy like Bobo Bigelow wear tall rubber boots.*

If nothing else, it did give me a marginal excuse to put off dealing with Dick Spencer.

My intention was to use my cousin's apartment in Westwood as home base while I was down in Los Angeles.

My mother's sister's oldest son, Bobby Senderowitz, was a more successful movie actor than I had ever been. He worked under the name Rob Sanders; you might have seen him in *Saving Private Ryan* unless you missed the first ten minutes.

Bobby was shooting a film somewhere in Mexico, another Hemingway adaptation if I'm not mistaken, and said I could use his place anytime I was in LA.

I thought about driving straight over to Alvarado Street but decided to stop at Bobby's to drop off my gear before heading over to look for the wild goose I would likely find at the address that Bobo had given me.

Maybe I would give Evelyn a call when I got to Bobby's place, tell her that I might have a lead on Harry's whereabouts.

Or maybe not.

I lit up a cigarette and pushed the Chevy to seventy-five, in a big hurry to get nowhere.

What greeted me when I walked into Bobby's apartment in Westwood was very different from what had waited for me at Dogtail's. Instead of a bottle of bourbon it was carrot juice and soy milk, instead of a two-quart aluminum saucepan it was an imported cappuccino machine, and then there were the photographs.

Bobby's apartment was plastered with family photos.

From photos on the mock fireplace mantel, to hung photographs of all sizes, to the collage covering most of the kitchen wall.

At the center of it all was the large framed portrait of our maternal grandfather, Louis Falco.

My grandfather had sailed to New York City from Sicily in 1915. He celebrated his fifth birthday on the ship that he, his mother, and his older brother had boarded in Liverpool. That same ship, the *Lusitania*, was sunk by a German U-boat on its return voyage a month later.

They had come to join his father, Giuseppi, who had arrived in New York in 1909 and would be seeing his son Louis for the first time. If America was the land of opportunity, it was also the land of what came to be known as the Falco gender curse. Giuseppi and his wife, Angela, had four more children, all girls. Their oldest son, Charlie, and his wife, Francesca, had three children, all girls. Louis and his wife, Josephine, had four children, all girls. Now don't get me wrong; my grandfather had nothing against girl children. But all hopes of perpetuating the Falco name ended with the birth of my Aunt Rosalie, Bobby's mother, in 1939. There have been many male children born into the family since then, but they all have names like O'Leary, Diamond, Senderowitz, and Leone. Not a Falco to be found. It was a tough blow to my grandfather, who, as most Italians do, placed great importance on the family name.

I'm just thankful that the old man had passed away before Cousin Bobby chose Sanders instead of Falco as his screen name.

I had once asked Darlene what she thought about changing the name of the business to Falco Investigation. She told me that if she ever started getting regular paychecks she might care more about what appeared in the upper left-hand corner.

SEVEN

Sometimes it's all in how you ask the question.

For instance.

If you want to know what time it is, don't ask, "Do you have the time?"

If you are remotely interested in a quick assessment of how a person is doing, don't ask, "What d'ya know?"

And never ask, "Did you get a haircut?" unless you want to hear that they were all cut.

Come to think of it, don't bring up haircuts at all.

When I had asked Bobo if there was a telephone at the address where he said I would find Harry Harding, Bigelow said that there was. When I asked him to write the phone number down on the paper napkin, he told me that he didn't know the phone number.

I showered and shaved, put on my last clean shirt, passed on the carrot juice, which was beginning to turn green, and pointed the Chevy toward Alvarado Street. The address was on Sixth and Alvarado, facing MacArthur Park. I pulled up in front and was almost out of the car when I heard the gunshot.

I ran up to the front door and found it locked. I used my elbow to break one of the small glass panes in the door, which by the way hurt like hell, and unlocked the door from the inside. I ran to the rear of the house and found the back door open. I peered out, but there was no one in sight. Then I heard moaning and looked down to find a man on the floor gushing blood. I saw that it was a head wound and didn't think that he would last long. I got down on the floor and hoped he would last just long enough.

"Harry Harding?" I asked.

"Harold Harding," he gasped.

Very helpful.

"Did you kill Jimmy Pigeon?" I asked.

"No," he said.

"Do you know who did?"

"No."

"Do you know who shot you?" I asked.

It took all of the energy he had left to answer.

"Yes," he said in a faint whisper. And then he died.

Sometimes it's all in how you ask the question.

I was planning to leave the scene after calling it in, but the model citizen with a Dick Tracy complex who was out front jotting down my license plate number changed my mind. I picked up the piece of paper I spotted lying at my feet. A claim ticket from a San Francisco dry cleaner's. I gave it a quick peek and stuffed it into my pocket.

I settled into a chair, lit a Camel, and waited for the police to arrive.

The way my luck had been going, I was not at all surprised when the first person to walk through the door was Lieutenant Boyle, LAPD Homicide.

"What d'ya know, Jake?" he asked.

"I've had better days, Ray. How are you?"

"No, I mean what do you know? Like, for example, who's the stiff?"

"Harold Harding."

"What a break. We've been looking all over for him."

"So I heard."

"Seems he popped your good friend Jimmy Pigeon."

"You think so?"

"Found his gun, prints and all, lying right at Jimmy's feet."

"How convenient."

"You sound skeptical."

"Hey, Lieutenant, what do I know?"

"That's what I'm trying to find out. Now me, I don't particularly like Harding for Jimmy's murder. I like the evidence, but I would be happier with a good motive. And as much as you'd like to think that you're a one-man crusade, I happen to be interested in who killed Pigeon. It's my job. And you're not making it easier. How did you find old Harry here?"

"Got a tip from Bobo Bigelow."

"What made you think a tip from that clown was worth your time?"

"Actually, I didn't, but there was nothing good on TV."

"That's clever, Jake. Think about this the next time you check the local listings: maybe if you had called me, Harry wouldn't be lying facedown in his own blood."

Boyle could be dramatic at times, but I couldn't deny the possibility. In fact, I couldn't say anything.

"I have to ask, Jake. Did you kill Harding?"

"Nope."

"Do you know who did? If the answer is yes, just give me a name; it'll save us some time."

I guess that's why Boyle was making the big bucks.

"Don't know."

"What did he say before he signed off?"

I had to admit Boyle was good.

"By the time I got to him he wasn't talking," I said.

I was embarrassed enough as it was.

"Were you being paid by his wife to find him?" Boyle asked.

"Lucky guess?"

"I hear things," he said. "Are you staying at the Red Rooster inn?"

Ray Boyle and I had a history, going back to my days with Jimmy Pigeon in Santa Monica. There's an inherent dislike of private investigators that most members of the law enforcement community seem happy to share. Guys who do what I do for a living are generally regarded by guys who do what Boyle does for a living as something stuck to the bottom of their shoe. And the feeling goes both ways. Ray and I somehow managed to keep our sparring free of physical contact.

It didn't hurt that I had put four hundred miles between us.

The first time I had run into Ray, I was on a stakeout.

I had been talking a lot about opening my own office and Jimmy suddenly took a week off. Since Jimmy was famous for never taking a break from work, I suspected that he was giving me a chance to get my feet wet. I wound up getting soaked.

I was hired by a guy who suspected that his girlfriend was unfaithful. He wanted me to find out where she was shacking up with the other man and let him know. It was not an unusual request, and I felt I was up to it. I followed her all over Santa Monica the next day and she finally led me to the Red Rooster on Route 405. I watched as a man inside one of the ground-level rooms let her in. I was at a pay phone outside the place, ready to call my client with the news, when I felt the gun in my ribs.

I slowly turned and saw the LAPD badge an inch from my nose. The detective motioned for me to follow him and I eagerly obliged. In his car I explained who I was and what I was doing there.

He told me that he thought Jimmy Pigeon had better sense.

Ray Boyle went on to explain that my client was a drug dealer under investigation and the dealer's girlfriend was an undercover narcotics officer meeting her partner to make her weekly report.

After making sure that the dealer wasn't tailing her.

And Detective Boyle told me, in no uncertain terms, that I could have gotten them both killed.

I didn't answer the phone for the remainder of the time Jimmy was away, and I put off setting up shop on my own for another six months.

Ray never let me forget it. He always managed to squeeze the word *rooster* in whenever we crossed paths.

"You said you'd be happier if you could find a good motive, Ray," I said, taking it on the chin. "Come up with any ideas?"

"Oh, all of a sudden you want to play show-and-tell. I'm on this, Jake. You know me. I don't like unsolved homicides; it's bad for the résumé. Let me worry about Pigeon and Harding. At the risk of sounding less than cordial, it's none of your business."

I wanted to believe he was wrong about that.

"I think I'll be going," I said.

"Would you like to use the phone before you head out?" he asked.

"Can I call Mexico? Tell my cousin Bobby that his carrot juice went bad?"

"Thought you might want to tell your client that you located her husband."

Not particularly.

"Maybe I'll just let you break it to her,

Ray. You're so good at it."

"Maybe she already knows."

It had crossed my mind.

"What makes you say that?"

"I'm not all that sure how it works. Something to do with the tongue and the vocal cords, I would think."

OK, so I'll never learn.

"Did Vinnie Strings come down with you?" Ray asked.

"No, I left him up in San Francisco. Why do you ask?"

"I just thought he'd be itching to help find Jimmy's killer, being such a helpful kid and all. And thought he might be anxious to see how he did in Jimmy's will. Keep him away, Jake. Go back home and sit on him if you have to."

Unfortunately, it looked like it was too late for that.

"You asking me to get out of Dodge, Ray?"

"Keep me informed as to where I can find you, Jake. In case I need your help," he said.

Boyle had rubbing it in down to a science.

"Will do," I said, just wanting to get away from there.

I gave him my best imitation of a smile and headed for my car.

I was hungry and tired. I didn't have a

client anymore as far as I could see. It's not that I had no feelings about what happened to Harding — a bullet in the head is not a happy fate — but who killed Harry interested me most to the extent that it could tell me something about who killed Jimmy Pigeon.

As far as the notion that Ray Boyle had planted, that calling the police earlier might have saved Harry, I tried not to let it grow.

With both Jimmy and Harding out of the way, who decided if Walter Richman was going to get his greedy paws on Ex-Con.com? If Evelyn Harding wanted to sell, there was apparently nothing holding her back now. But for all I knew she could have been on Jimmy's side of that debate. I supposed I could ask her, but I really couldn't see why she would think it was any of my business.

I still needed to see Dick Spencer to find out who actually controlled Jimmy's interests. That's if Spencer had reason to think *that* was any of my business.

Maybe none of it was any of my fucking business.

Except that I wanted to make it my business. I wanted to find out who ended Jimmy's life and make sure that the guilty party didn't benefit from his death.

He would have done the same for me.

It's not that I didn't trust Boyle to follow all the leads, if he could do better than I had finding any. In fact, I was glad to hear that Ray was at least professionally curious.

Only I wasn't quite ready to become a nonparticipant.

I decided to go back to Plan A and pay a call on Dick Spencer. What the hell, I'd taken some lumps, but I could handle a little more abuse. I'm a pretty humble guy. The way things usually go with me, I've learned that it's my best bet.

And I still had it in mind to drop in on Evelyn Harding, Grace or no Grace.

I also decided that I had better grab something to eat before I went out social calling. I hadn't had much luck in that department lately, so I thought I'd play it safe and pick up a pizza. I took a large sausage-and-black-olive to go from Pete's Original on Broadway and brought it back to my cousin Bobby's place.

When I arrived I found Vinnie Strings waiting for me at Bobby's door.

EIGHT

"What the fuck are you doing down here, Vinnie?"

"Would you believe I came to help you eat that pie?"

"I'm ready to believe just about anything within reason, Vinnie. But somehow I don't believe you have it in you."

I shoved him through the door, ahead of me and the pizza.

Fifteen minutes later I was trying to figure out how to make a cappuccino using soy milk and Vinnie Strings was reaching for his fourth slice.

"I'm glad you finally decided to get the mustard-and-beer residue off your Oakland Raiders jacket," I said.

"Huh?"

"You must have dropped this back at Alvarado Street," I said, reaching into my pocket and pulling out the dry-cleaning ticket.

"Jesus, Jake. I can explain."

"I can hardly wait."

"I felt bad about letting you come down here alone. I figured you were just too proud to ask for help."

That'll be the day.

"So?"

"So I toyed with the idea of coming down to give you a hand. I called this guy who gets cheap plane tickets."

"Let me guess. Bobo Bigelow?"

"Yeah. So Bigelow fixes me up, even gets me a fantastic deal on a rental car at the airport."

"That death trap out front?"

"For nine ninety-five a day I'll take my chances. Anyway, while Bobo has my ear he starts filling it with all this business about Jimmy leaving me a bundle and how I'd better watch out Harry Harding doesn't screw me out of it."

"Did you confirm this alleged windfall with Spencer?"

"Couldn't find the man."

"So Bobo tells you where you can find Harding."

"Yeah, he gives me the place on Mac-Arthur Park."

Good old tight-lipped Bobo Bigelow. He tips me to Harry's hideout, promises me an

71

exclusive, and turns right around and gives Harding up to Vinnie. The question was, Who else did he tell?

"And you drop over to have a heart-to-heart with Harry."

"Exactly. It's amazing how you can read me, Jake."

"Like a comic book, kid. So what happened with Harding?"

"He told me not to worry. He said nothing was going to happen with the Web company without his say-so, and mine if I had a significant piece of Jimmy's end. He said we could work it out as soon as he cleared up the little mess he was in, being a murder suspect and all."

"And you were satisfied?"

"He didn't seem like a bad guy. I guess I wanted to believe him."

"So you shook hands on it and left?"

"More or less."

"And he was still standing?"

"What do you mean?"

"Someone put a bullet in him."

"Is he dead?"

"Dead as Abe Lincoln."

"Jesus, Jake! What do we do now?"

"If you can tear yourself away from that pizza, we could hunt down Dick Spencer and find out if you're the benefactee that your travel agent seems to think you are. Want to try a nondairy latté?"

"Man, am I glad you picked up that dry-cleaning stub."

"Better me than Constable Boyle."

"Boyle was there?"

"Big as life."

"Yeah, buddy, better you than Boyle," said Vinnie. "The jacket wouldn't fit him anyway."

"Don't 'buddy' me, Strings. I am very disappointed in you."

"I'm sorry, Jake. I just wanted to protect the eggs in my basket."

"I wouldn't count the chickens just yet. Are you ready to get out of here or what?"

"Can I get that espresso to go?"

"Need a buzz?"

"Are you kidding? I use the caffeine to come down."

"Would you do me a favor, Vinnie?"

"Anything, Jake. Just name it."

"Scrape that hunk of sausage off your tooth; it's freaking me out."

I could hear him working at it as he followed me out to the car.

When we walked into Dick Spencer's office suite, an accurate description of the rooms in this case, his receptionist was what I could best describe as leery.

When Vinnie cruised right up to her desk, gave her a broad smile, and asked her if he had any black olive on his teeth it didn't help to ease her mind.

"Dick around?" I asked.

"Do you have an appointment, sir?" She had to choke out the last word.

"Tell him Jake Diamond is here to see him. I think he'll squeeze us in."

She announced my presence on the speakerphone as if discussing a rash with her dermatologist. I could hear Spencer tell her that he would be right out and would she please block the exit door to make sure that I didn't escape.

A minute later Spencer appeared in the reception area.

"Did you bring your checkbook?" he said.

Nice way to begin.

"I dropped it on my way into the building and it bounced down Wilshire."

"Who's your friend with the oregano on his collar?"

"Vinnie Stradivarius. Name mean anything to you?" I asked.

"Sure does. Come on back to my inner sanctum. Vinnie here can float you a loan for your alimony debt and a couple of new ties."

"You think he means I'm coming into

some money, Jake?" asked Vinnie as we followed Spencer down the corridor.

If it were anyone else I would have figured it for rhetorical.

"Have a seat, boys," said Spencer when we arrived at his office. "I'm going to take a wild guess that you're here to find out if Jimmy Pigeon left a last will and testament."

"And to think that some people have the nerve to suggest that a law degree from the University of Martinique isn't worth every square inch of paper it's printed on," I said.

"That's pretty funny coming from a PI who couldn't find his own mouth without zeroing in on it with the neck of a bourbon bottle."

Dick Spencer and I had mutual feelings for each other.

I'd often suspected that it was Spencer who put Sally up to sending me the spousal maintenance statement every month.

"Why not simply tell us about Jimmy's will and then just throw us out?"

"Don't you want to congratulate me first? I'm getting married."

"Who's the lucky girl?" I asked.

Not that I cared. I just wanted to put a face on the poor woman so that I could picture who to feel sorry for.

"I'll give you a hint. You won't have to

make support payments anymore, not that it really changes anything."

The thought that my ex-wife, Sally, was the poor woman in question was as revolting as the stringy piece of mozzarella and tomato sauce hanging off Vinnie's sleeve.

Speaking of Vinnie, he finally mustered up enough courage to jump into the conversation.

"I don't get it," he said. "Are we talking about Jimmy's will or what? You guys lost me at the part about the bourbon bottle."

Vinnie wasn't very bright.

"That's wonderful news, Dick," I said, anxious to get past it. "Now how about telling Vinnie if he hit the jackpot before the kid crawls out of his skin."

"Five grand and a 1985 Olds Ninety-eight," Spencer said.

"Vinnie gets five thousand dollars and Jimmy's car?"

"Or to put it a third way, one-half of Pigeon's life insurance benefit and the gas-guzzler. The other half, five thousand dollars if you're not up to doing the arithmetic yourself, goes to you, Diamond. Minus the twenty-five hundred you owe Sally. Plus all of Jimmy's surveillance gear, which I would guess consists mostly of tin cans connected with string."

"That's it?" said Vinnie Stradivarius.

Vinnie was a stickler for clarification.

"Jimmy had twenty thousand in an individual retirement account which he left to Tina Bella Pazzo. He thought she might need a little grubstake if she decided to put some distance between herself and the maniac she calls a husband. And there's some furniture and clothing that looks like it came off the set of *Saturday Night Fever*, but you'll have to fight it out with the Salvation Army over custody."

"How about Jimmy's half of Ex-Con dot com?" asked Vinnie.

"It went a different route entirely."

"Which route would that be, Dick?" I asked.

"I'm not obligated to say anything about that if the party in question prefers to remain anonymous."

"I'm lost again," said Vinnie. "Who gets Jimmy's half of the business?"

I gave Vinnie a look that shut him up. It wouldn't last long.

"Look, Dick. That information could be a lead to who killed Jimmy."

"Detective Boyle had the same idea when he dropped in on me a few days ago. I told him what he needed to know. I feel as if I've done my civic duty."

"And Boyle told you not to talk to me?"

"He didn't have to, Diamond."

"When can I get my five grand?" asked Vinnie. He seemed to have lost interest in the larger issues.

"Keep your shirt on, Vinnie," I said.

"Look, Diamond. I'm sure this will come as no surprise, but I dislike you. A lot. However, I did like Jimmy Pigeon. And I somehow believe that your interest in all of this has to do with what happened to Jimmy and not what he left behind. So I'll tell you this much, just to save you from your own sordid imagination."

I was interested enough not to interrupt Dick's eloquent preface. I could at least give him a ten count.

"Jimmy had a wife," Spencer went on. "He walked out on her years ago. She remarried soon after and she was recently widowed. Jimmy had me sending her money every few months to help her out. Jimmy named her in his will. And that's all I will say about it."

"You won't tell me who or where she is?"

"No, I won't. Why should I, when your good pal Jimmy Pigeon wouldn't even tell you about her?"

Spencer had a good point. And it stuck right in.

"I want to be sure I'm straight on this, Dick. Evelyn Harding and Jimmy's ex-wife split the million if they sell to Walter Richman?"

If I didn't come up with a motive soon I would be back up at Willie Dogtail's begging him for more of his coffee.

"I wouldn't count Harry Harding out yet," Spencer said, "but that's beside the point."

"You can count Harry out; he took a bullet in the head earlier today."

"Are you serious?"

"As a heart attack. What's beside the point?"

"Richman withdrew his offer."

"Oh," I said.

"Oh?" Spencer said.

I rebounded before Vinnie could open his mouth again.

"So is the business worth anything?" I asked.

"That's not my area, Diamond. I was Pigeon's lawyer, not his business adviser. You'd have to talk to whoever he used for financial counsel."

"And who would that have been?"

"There you go again, Diamond. You were his good buddy. You tell me."

Spencer just couldn't resist the extra thrust.

"Thanks a lot, Dick."

"It's nothing, Diamond," he said.

I couldn't have said it better.

Before we left Dick Spencer he told Vinnie to drop by on Monday afternoon to pick up a check for $5,000. He also told me I could pick up my twenty-five hundred.

I told him that he and Sally could keep it for a wedding present. Invest in earplugs and body armor.

I was having a hard time reconciling how out of touch I had been with Jimmy. Even inside the joint, Sam the Sham knew more about what was going on with Pigeon than I had.

At the front desk I asked Dick's receptionist if I could use the phone, which she reluctantly allowed. She likely had a spray can of Lysol handy for when I was done. I called Willie Dogtail to make sure it would be all right to unload Vinnie on him for the weekend. I had some thinking to do, with minimal distraction.

It was still early, so I treated Vinnie to dinner just to kill time. We sat in a diner at San Pedro and Temple near city hall for more than two hours. In silence.

Vinnie was perceptive enough for a change to sense my mood and was afraid to open his mouth.

I really had nothing to say.

"Dogtail says you're welcome to hang at his place until Monday if you like, Vin," I said as we pulled up in front of my cousin Bobby's place just after eight. "You can play the ponies on the weekend and you'll love his coffee."

"I don't mind staying to give you a leg up, Jake."

"Thanks, Vinnie," I said, "but no thanks."

"OK, pal. You'll call if you need me, right?"

"Absolutely."

He got out of the Impala, got into his rental, and drove off.

I got out and started for Bobby's door, but I veered toward the corner package store, thinking I could use a little help from George Dickel to work out my next move.

After three straight shots I knew that I wasn't going to work out much at all.

Somehow I did manage to conclude that although I was done with trying to locate Harry Harding for his wife, I had no better idea than to pay Evelyn a visit.

After the fourth shot I decided that it would wait until morning.

I picked up the Dickens book and took it into the bedroom with the bottle.

Paris. 1775.

A keg of wine had fallen off a carriage and spilled its contents onto the cobblestoned street. Bystanders of all ages and social classes rushed over and began collecting the liquid with cupped hands, ceramic bowls, spoons, and handkerchiefs. A woman sopped up wine with her scarf and squeezed drops into the mouth of her hungry infant.

It was a disheartening depiction of the unquenchable thirst and despair in the city. Not much different from the feeling I got being back in Los Angeles.

Jimmy Pigeon had loved LA.

I thought about the first case that Jimmy had brought me in on.

A friend had come to Jimmy, worried about his wife.

The woman worked as assistant to a Los Angeles city councilman. She had overheard a conversation between the councilman and a local contractor.

The council was about to decide on bids for the construction of a new piece of freeway. The contractor was there to buy a vote.

It was nothing new, it went on all the time, and everyone turned deaf and blind and filled their pockets.

The woman was afraid for her job, Jimmy's friend was afraid for his wife, and my advice would have been to forget that she had heard anything.

But Jimmy Pigeon had LA in mind. It was his home, and he took the sanctity of his home seriously. So Jimmy went to work.

The contractor lost the bid, the councilman lost his job, the woman won his seat on the council, and Jimmy Pigeon slept easy.

"I love LA, Jake, as much as I've ever loved anything," Jimmy told me. "She makes me feel alive. I tried to leave once, but she pulled me back. I do what I can to keep her honest."

I don't know. I suppose that being in the midst of so many walking dead could make anyone with a touch of self-esteem feel alive. And Jimmy had more than a little self-esteem.

Jimmy Pigeon was sure of who he was and pleased with himself. He loved his life so much that it rubbed off on everyone he came in contact with.

Almost everyone.

There must have been at least one person who Jimmy couldn't win over, and somehow that person had gotten close enough to Jimmy to put him under the ground.

I closed the Dickens book and took another long pull from the bourbon bottle. I lay back in the bed. It was a lot more welcoming than the motel bed in Obispo and the futon at Willie Dogtail's place, though I could have done without the silk sheets.

I set down the bottle and picked up the TV remote.

I found an old John Garfield movie.

Lana Turner was talking Garfield into helping murder her husband while making him think that it was his idea all the time.

I knew how it ended, and before it did I was out cold.

NINE

I woke up wondering whether George Dickel drank much of his own bourbon and, if he did, how he ever managed to run a business. I could smell the coffee brewing in the kitchen. I decided to check it out before hitting the shower and found a business card leaning against the coffeemaker. On the back of the card was written: *"Ran out to get some half-and-half."* I turned it over to where it simply read: "Detective R. Boyle, LAPD." I jumped into the shower, hoping that Ray would at least come back with some doughnuts.

When I returned to the kitchen, Boyle was sitting at the table with a mug of coffee in one hand and a chocolate-dipped in the other. Good man. I helped myself to a cup, added some cream, and grabbed a honey-glazed.

"Don't care for soy milk, Ray?" I said.

"I just came from visiting a friend of yours at LA General Hospital."

"Could you be more specific?" I asked.

Not that I had that many friends.

"Dick Spencer."

"Did he say who put him there?"

"Wouldn't say, but I heard you dropped in on him yesterday. I thought you could enlighten me."

"No idea. He going to be all right?"

"Depends on whether you think he was ever all right."

"Point well taken. Sorry I can't help you. How'd you find me?"

"Yahoo! Search."

"Cute."

"I wasn't trying to be. I was just wondering why everyone you visit down here has such bad luck," he said.

"I hope you figure it out."

"I was going to suggest you head back up to San Francisco before you put a hex on anyone else."

"Haven't we been through this before, Ray?"

"More times than I care to remember. How's that doughnut?"

"Very good. Krispy Kreme?"

"Safeway. Your pal Vinnie still around?"

"I'd bet you could find him at Santa Anita at post time. How did you know he was down here?"

"You just told me. Don't forget to take him along with you when you head back."

"Spencer said that Jimmy had a wife, way back when, and that he'd been sending money. Do you think she figures in this somehow?"

"I don't think so," Boyle said, and then to assure me that it was all he had to say about it he repeated, "Don't forget to take Strings along with you when you head back."

"Sure. You can take the rest of the doughnuts back to the precinct."

I had a strong hunch about who had danced on Dick Spencer's head, and not two minutes after Boyle left, leaving the half-and-half and taking the doughnuts, my theory was confirmed.

When I opened the door I was instantly reminded of why Jimmy Pigeon had taken the risk.

"Can I come in, Jake?"

"Sure, Tina," I said, letting her pass. "Care for some coffee?"

"That would be great. Have any doughnuts?"

"Half a honey-glazed; help yourself," I said, following her into the kitchen.

Tina Bella Pazzo was a handsome woman. I poured her a cup and sat across from her at the kitchen table.

"What's up, Tina?"

"I need some help, Jake."

"I haven't been too lucky for people lately, Tina."

She was nervously playing table hockey with the half-eaten doughnut.

"I don't know who else to turn to, Jake," she said.

How come that one always worked with me?

"I'll listen."

"Crazy Al is looking for me and I don't think it's to bring me flowers. I was pretty well hid, but I think Dick Spencer may have leaked my location."

"Well, for what it's worth, it looks like Dick did hold out for quite a while."

"Yeah, I heard that Al's gorilla really tattooed him."

"How'd you find me?"

"Spencer. He called me from the hospital to warn me. He had to write it down for the nurse to read, since his jaw is wired shut."

When I'd told Spencer where I would be staying, I didn't expect it would become LA's key attraction. I guess Dick wrote it down for the nurse to read to Ray Boyle also.

"That was sweet of him. What do you expect me to do, Tina?"

"I just need a place to lay low until my money from Jimmy comes through and I can disappear to Mexico or somewhere."

"Did Al kill Jimmy?"

"No. Someone beat him to it. Al has a good alibi. Unfortunately, he was with me when Jimmy was killed."

"Any ideas about who the somebody who beat him to it might be? I hear that you and Jimmy were compromising Al's conjugal rights. Jimmy talk in his sleep?"

"Jimmy didn't talk to me about cases, Jake. You should know that."

"He ever talk to you about a wife?"

"And Jimmy didn't talk about other women. It was none of my business. But I can't picture Jimmy as a married man."

I guessed that Jimmy couldn't picture it, either.

"It was ancient history," I said.

"He didn't talk history, either. He was more interested in anatomy. Are you going to help me, Jake?"

"OK, Tina, for Jimmy's sake. You can stay at my place up in San Francisco while I'm down here. I'll try to get Spencer to slip your inheritance to me and I'll bring it up. I hope you realize that you're putting me in danger."

"I thought that danger was your middle name, Jake."

"No, Tina. That was Jimmy's middle name. I'll call Darlene and tell her to expect you; she'll give you the keys to my flat. Go ahead; finish that doughnut."

After Tina left, I gave Darlene a call up at the office. I asked her to set Tina up at my place and then stay far away from her. I told Darlene that if anyone dropped by at the office and strongly insisted that she let on where Tina was holed up she shouldn't hesitate coming clean. I had my priorities in order.

"Anything exciting going on up there?" I asked.

"A couple of calls, but I had to put them off. I tried to find Vinnie to cover, but thankfully he's not around."

"Yeah, I know. He's down here."

"That must delight you. When will you be back?"

"Soon, I hope."

"Are you making any money, at least?"

"As a matter of fact, no."

"You're going to blow your shot at Bay Area Businessman of the Year."

"Five years in a row."

"Jake."

"Yes, Darlene."

"Be careful."

"You, too. Remember if it's between you

or Tina getting hurt . . ."

"Gotcha," she said.

"I'll stay in touch," I said.

"Please do. By the way."

"Yeah."

"You have some mail piling up."

"Anything that isn't a bill?"

"One or two pieces. Want me to open them?"

"Sure. Open everything. Let me know if there's anything important. I'll be here at my cousin's place unless you hear different or unless anyone asks."

I thought about phoning Evelyn Harding to announce my intention to call on her but decided not to give her the opportunity to tell me not to bother. Judging from the way I had been forewarned by my visitors since I'd been there, I figured that in Los Angeles Emily Post was pretty much ignored. Vinnie and Tina had popped in unannounced, and Boyle hadn't even bothered to knock.

I looked up the address of the Harding residence in the phone book and dressed for the occasion. I really did need to get a few more ties. I borrowed one of Bobby's.

I hopped into my car, downing the last of the honey-glazed that Tina had only pushed around, and directed the Chevy out to Beverly Hills.

As I headed out Wilshire toward 405 North I tried to review what I knew, figuring it would be easier than trying to inventory what I didn't know.

The latest revelation had been Crazy Al's defense. The last person who would want to clear Pazzo of anything was Tina, so if she put him somewhere else when Jimmy was capped the alibi was ironclad. Well, that was one less suspect in Pigeon's murder. For that matter, I could eliminate Tina as a suspect as well, unless she and Crazy Al were in it together. That was too scary a thought, so I let it pass.

I might have felt I was making progress if I didn't know better.

I didn't like Bobo Bigelow or Vinnie Strings for it, either. Bobo really didn't have that big a gripe, and I believed that Vinnie really cared for Jimmy. And if nothing else, I didn't consider either of them smart enough to get the drop on Pigeon.

As far as Harry Harding being the shooter, I could eliminate him just because I knew that nothing ever comes to me that easily.

And according to Dick Spencer, Walter Richman seemed to have lost interest in Ex-Con.com.

When I approached the Hills I wondered

if I would find Evelyn Harding at home and, if so, she would want to talk. I wasn't quite sure about the reason I would give her for my ambush: "Oh, by the way, Evelyn, did you happen to murder Jimmy Pigeon and your husband for the dough?" Being unprepared was getting to be a bad habit with me. I finally decided as I reached the cul-de-sac where Evelyn Harding lived that I would take an indirect approach and wing it.

As I pulled up in front of the huge house I adjusted Bobby's tie, trying to force it into matching the sport jacket I was wearing. It wasn't going to happen. I took a deep breath and headed up the stairs, dwarfed by the columns on each side of the entrance. I would simply say that I dropped by to give my condolences and then play dumb. It shouldn't be difficult; I had playing dumb down to an art form.

I rang the doorbell. I could swear that the chimes played *"Tara's Theme."* A minute later I heard the door being opened from the inside.

The young woman who materialized in the doorway made Tina Bella look like Woody Allen. Long blond hair with a skinny braid hanging down the left side. Deeply tanned skin that made Sophia Loren look pale in comparison. The white bikini she was wearing accentuated the obvious.

If she said that her name was Lolita it wouldn't have surprised me a bit.

"Nice tie," she said, and then added, "I'm at least eighteen."

I felt two hundred.

"I was looking for Evelyn Harding," I managed to choke out.

She was doing something with her eyes that was mildly distracting.

"Mom is out back; we were getting ready to take a dip. Did you bring your bathing suit?"

"I left it in my other jacket. Do you think you could tell your mother that Jake Diamond is here to see her?"

"Is she expecting you?"

"No."

"Great. Mom hates surprises. Come on in; I'll take you back."

"Maybe I should just wait here."

"Suit yourself," she said; it sounded like a question. "I'll tell Mom that you've happened by. In case you were wondering, my name is Trouble."

She gave a little laugh and headed to the back of the house.

I stood fidgeting at the door. If that was Evelyn Harding's daughter it sure shot the hell out of genetic theory.

And by the way, didn't mother and daughter have arrangements to attend to? After all, Harry had been dearly departed for less than twenty-four hours and these gals were frolicking around the pool. Was it possible that they were unaware? I was counting on Boyle to handle notification. If I was here to break the news I was more unprepared than even I had imagined.

What Evelyn Harding said when she appeared at the door eased my mind.

I think.

"I heard you found my husband, Mr. Diamond," she said.

"Yes. And a little too late, I'm afraid. I'm sorry."

"Is there something that I can do for you, Mr. Diamond? Are you covered on your fees?"

That pretty much answered the question as to Evelyn Harding's interest in sustaining our relationship.

And she never did get around to calling me Jake.

"Yes, Mrs. Harding, I'm covered," I said and then nonchalantly added, "Do you have any idea who may have killed your husband?"

What the hell, couldn't hurt to ask.

"I already answered that question for Detective Boyle, and I don't really understand your interest, but if it will help you any, I have no idea."

Great help. I figured that asking about plans for her share of the Internet business wouldn't get me very far, either.

"Working out the funeral details poolside?" I said, regretting it the moment it slipped out.

"Mr. Diamond, how I manage my grief is really none of your concern, now is it?"

"No, it isn't. I apologize."

"Good day."

"I was wondering if I might speak with Grace."

"What about?"

"I know that she kept in touch with Jimmy. I thought that maybe she could tell me something about what he'd been up to."

"Is Grace suspected of something, Mr. Diamond?"

A curious question.

"No, of course not."

"Grace left town, Mr. Diamond. Before your friend Jimmy was killed."

I decided not to ask where Grace left to or why Evelyn made it a point to say when she left. My foot was already sore from all the dead horses I had kicked lately. I reiterated my condolences to Evelyn Harding as she closed the door in my face. It had been three days since she first walked into my office and I was no closer to discovering who killed Jimmy Pigeon or why.

I climbed into the Chevy and started the engine.

I turned on the radio and lit a cigarette.

I sadly realized that the worst part of trying to solve the case was not having Jimmy there to help me.

And then I remembered that in some respects he was.

And that it was time I started listening to what Jimmy had to say.

TEN

One of the first pieces of advice Jimmy Pigeon ever gave me, after "always insist on a fee in advance and never argue with a man holding a gun," was to trust my instincts.

"What if my instincts are consistently wrong?" I'd asked.

"That's how you tell if you're in the wrong business," he'd said.

I'd actually had similar advice from my college drama instructor.

My instincts were telling me that Walter Richman figured in somehow. I decided that I would pay him a visit.

I also felt that talking with Jimmy Pigeon's long-lost wife might be more revealing than Spencer or Boyle thought it might be. The chances of getting the information out of Detective Boyle were slim to none. Instead, I would drop by the hospital and pull it out from between Dick Spencer's wired teeth.

When I got back to Bobby's place I realized

that I was hungry, having gone half the day without anything to eat but a doughnut. There was nothing in my cousin's Kenmore that even vaguely resembled lunch, so I took the phone number off a menu stuck on the refrigerator door and called in for delivery of a chicken dish named after some Chinese general.

After ordering the food I stared at the telephone trying to decide whether to call Walter Richman or check the visiting hours at LA General.

To look at me you would have thought I was trying to decide whether or not to drop the bomb on Nagasaki. Before I could make up my mind the phone rang, nearly causing me to swallow my cigarette.

Darlene.

"Just checking to see if you're OK," she said.

"I wish I knew, Darlene," I said. "Did Tina Bella get in touch?"

"Not yet."

"Remember, when she shows up, put her in my place and tell her not to answer the door or the phone and give her up if you have to."

"Got it."

"Anything good in the mail?"

"Another letter from Dick Spencer about back alimony and an invitation to try *Time*

99

magazine at sixty-eight cents an issue with a free pocket thesaurus thrown in."

"Trash them both."

"Today's mail should be here soon; maybe you'll get that two-point-nine percent Visa Platinum Card application you've been hoping for."

"Funny."

"What would you like to do about the rent here?"

"I thought we paid the rent for this month a few days ago."

"I was thinking about next month; it's already the twenty-eighth."

Darlene could go on like that forever. Fortunately, I had to excuse myself to answer the door for the restaurant delivery.

The general who my meal was named after must have fought during the Boxer Rebellion, because the vegetables tasted like they were picked around 1900. I had to fish around for the chicken, which was scarce, and wound up with what was basically a lunch of yesterday's warmed-over rice. The broccoli and bamboo shoots went into the garbage disposal. I'd have done better with the tofu in Bobby's cheese compartment.

I called Walter Richman.

"Richman International, Ms. Fairbanks speaking."

I could see that humility wasn't going to be one of Walter's strong points.

"Good afternoon. This is Jake Diamond for Mr. Richman."

"Mr. Richman is out of town, Mr. Diamond. Mr. Alster is here taking his calls if you would like to speak with him."

I couldn't see why not.

"Why not," I said.

"Fine; it'll be just a minute. Can I get you a cup of coffee while you wait?"

"Can you do that?"

"Just kidding. Please hold."

You know how sometimes when you speak to someone on the phone it makes you kind of curious to meet the person?

And then again sometimes not.

"Mr. Diamond, how can Richman International be of service to you today?"

Alster sounded like he was practicing his Orson Welles impersonation.

"I had been hoping to talk with Mr. Richman about Ex-Con dot com."

"We've withdrawn our offer on that particular company, Mr. Diamond."

"So I heard. I was just curious about some of the details," I said. "How the offer came about. Why the loss of interest. Who Mr. Richman had been dealing with. That sort of thing."

"This may sound strange, but actually, Mr. Richman wouldn't know very much about it. He leaves the small transactions to his associates."

He was talking about a million dollars as if it were chump change.

"Well, how about I talk to the associate who was negotiating the deal before it fell through?" I said. "Just a few simple questions, a few minutes on the telephone."

I was wondering when he was going to ask me exactly who I was and what business it was to me.

"I think that I can help you with your questions, Mr. Diamond. It was my decision to pull out of the deal."

"Fair enough," I said.

"However, I'd much rather speak in person and away from the office if it's convenient. Have you eaten?"

"Not really."

"Could I buy you lunch at the Beverly Hills Hotel?"

I was guessing he could.

"I could meet you there in an hour," I said.

"Terrific," he said. "I'll look forward to seeing you then."

I was afraid that I might be somewhat underdressed for lunch at the Beverly Hills

102

Hotel. I would have borrowed one of Bobby's sport jackets, but he was considerably smaller than I was. Feasibly one of the reasons he went into acting.

I thought I might find another of his ties that would match my jacket a little better, but I couldn't find one with a paisley or Yosemite Sam pattern in his wardrobe.

I decided I would have to go as I was. Screw them if they couldn't take a joke.

When I reached the hotel restaurant, a man in a tuxedo, who didn't hesitate to identify himself as the maître d', asked me what I wanted as if I had a vacuum cleaner under my arm. He had a British accent that he overplayed like an Iowa high school kid doing Lear. When I told him that I was there to join Mr. Alster for lunch he asked if I would care to borrow a jacket from the hotel. I politely declined. He solemnly led me to Alster's table. When he pulled out the chair and motioned for me to sit down I had a momentary fear that he wouldn't push it in behind me.

Alster hadn't arrived yet.

A waiter came up asking if I would care for a drink. I ordered a double shot of Jack Daniel's, sure that asking for Dickel would be misunderstood. He walked off with all the grace of a man with a rod up his ass. He must have taken walking lessons from the maître d'.

To kill time I played a game we used to play on long car trips with my parents. But instead of counting out-of-state license plates I counted Rolexes.

Alster came up to the table just as the waiter was bringing my drink. He put out his hand to me, squeezed mine a bit too hard when I accepted the handshake, and turned to the waiter.

"I'll have the usual, Clive," he said.

Nice name. I tried to guess what the maître d' called himself. I would have laid ten to one on Bentley or Jeeves. I looked up at Alster and he had a smile on his face that looked crocheted on. He sat down.

"Drink up, Mr. Diamond. No need to wait; we're not all that formal here."

His four-hundred-dollar Canali suit could have fooled me.

"I can hold out, Mr. Alster. Perhaps while we're waiting for your usual you can begin telling me about Ex-Con dot com."

"Call me Ted. Wouldn't you like to look at the menu first?"

"I'll let you order for me, Ted. I'm sure you know what's best here and besides, I don't think I could lift the thing."

"Very well, Mr. Diamond, what can I help you with?"

Hallelujah.

Just then the waiter arrived with Alster's drink. Ted asked Clive for a couple of filet mignons and a large Caesar salad. There was no general's name attached to the lunch order.

The food came almost immediately. That might have surprised me if the filet didn't look as if it had never touched the grill.

Ted Alster managed to remain precise and articulate between mouthfuls of raw steak and salad anchovies the size of brook trout.

I listened and looked on in horror.

Among other things, Richman International bought up small companies and re-sold them at a profit. Richman himself was busy with his film interests and left the small stuff to his highly qualified staff of corporate advisers.

One of the other corporate advisers working deals for Richman had apparently made an offer for Ex-Con.com. Harry Harding had called the office to speak to him, he wasn't available, and Alster took the call.

Harding told Alster that he was working out a little disagreement with Jimmy and that they would need more time before signing off on the sale. Alster asked Harding a few questions about the company and said he would pass the message on.

"I did some exploration and it seemed to me that the offer was out of line with what Mr. Harding's business was worth. I called Mr. Harding and told him that we had decided to withdraw the offer."

"Did you tell him why?"

"Not exactly. I didn't want to discourage him. I told Mr. Harding that we couldn't wait for them to work out their differences, that we had other transactions to move on."

"You're aware that both Harding and his partner have been murdered?" I said.

"Yes, I heard about that."

"Any ideas about that?"

"Not the slightest, Mr. Diamond. Why in the world would I?"

"And you never spoke with Harding's partner, Jimmy Pigeon?"

"No. We never got that far. I just hope that any animosity that the offer may have created between the two men had nothing to do with their tragic deaths."

Very neatly put.

"I would still like to speak with your associate, Mr. Alster. Ask him why he thought Ex-Con dot com was worth a million dollars in the first place."

"I'm afraid that I can't reveal his identity, Mr. Diamond."

"Why is that?"

"Because we're looking into that very question ourselves, and we would prefer to keep it in-house."

"When you say 'we,' are you including Mr. Richman?"

"I feel it would be best not to bother Mr. Richman with it until I know more about the details. It could simply have been a matter of poor judgment or inadequate research on the part of our associate. Until I can be certain, I prefer not to worry Mr. Richman and I want to avoid any damaging speculation or publicity."

"Mr. Alster, Jimmy Pigeon was a friend of mine. If the information you're keeping from me, whatever the reason, turns out to have anything to do with his death it won't sit well with me."

I didn't like the guy. And it wasn't just the way he ate.

Speaking of which, I hadn't touched a bite.

I thanked Alster, not quite knowing what for, and left the table.

As I passed the maître d' on the way out I told him to put the meal on my tab. I wanted to tell him that if he wanted a tip I would suggest he get out of the business. I did tip the kid who brought my car. He was so in love with the Impala that I wanted to run right over to see Dick Spencer and put the kid in my will.

Come to think of it, seeing Spencer was next on my short list.

I headed over to LA General.

I wanted to know who had inherited Jimmy's share of the company and what it might really be worth. Dick Spencer was an idiot, but he wasn't stupid. He had to know something about the value of the inheritance.

Another thought hit me. Regardless of its value, was the company worth owning?

Being a part-owner of Ex-Con.com had proven to be bad for one's health.

And the new owners, Evelyn Harding and Jimmy Pigeon's ex-wife, whoever and wherever she might be, weren't necessarily immune.

Of course with all of these musings cluttering my mind I totally neglected the obvious. So when I approached Spencer's hospital room I was caught by surprise when my ex-wife walked out the door. It was like being shocked to find Jack Nicholson at a Lakers game.

"He's asleep," she said. "Let me buy you a cup of coffee."

Sadness and guilt hit me like a garbage truck.

"Sure, Sally," I said. "You look great."

ELEVEN

I'll never forget the first time I laid eyes on Sally French.

Sally came into my San Francisco office shortly after I had opened shop. My first client. Jimmy Pigeon had sent her to me; she was looking to find her mother.

I was no expert in genealogy, but I was able to track down Mrs. Wanda Temple through an acquaintance in Adoption Services. Mrs. Temple had given Sally up for adoption at birth, when Wanda was a sixteen-year-old unmarried high school student. At twenty-one Wanda married millionaire Byron Temple. Temple had made his money in the import/export business and died when his Lear jet failed to clear Mount Abel in Los Padres National Forest. The Temples had no children. Wanda became intent on finding her long-lost daughter after Temple's plane went down and, as fate would have it, Sally had made up her mind to try locating her mother at about the same time. The coincidence served to make my job a lot easier.

Sally French was a knockout. She worked in a department store in Pleasant Hill, an upper-middle-class town east of San Francisco, but she could easily have been a fashion model or even a film actress. She had the looks that render acting ability unimportant. When she first walked into my office I was almost ready to give up the idea of private investigation and become her agent.

Shortly into the two months it took me to locate Wanda Temple, Sally and I began an affair.

Not very smart, but I wasn't intellectualizing much in those days.

When Sally and Wanda were finally reunited, both women were madly in love with me for helping to bring them together. It was a little too much admiration to turn my back on. Sally and I were soon married; Jimmy Pigeon was my best man. Sally and I moved into a house that Wanda had purchased for us near the Presidio.

Things were fine until Sally began recommending that I get out of the private investigation business. The vocation that had helped to locate her wealthy mother was no

111

longer worthy of her new husband. She had the dubious honor of being my first client and would have liked to be my last. Sally wasted little time making her feelings known.

Sally wanted me to go to work for Bytemp Enterprises, Byron Temple's corporation, which Wanda inherited total ownership of after Temple's death. Sally jumped into Bytemp with both feet. She enrolled in a business degree program at San Francisco State.

I wasn't as eager to take the plunge. I enjoyed my work too much. Sally went from disappointment to resentment in record time. By the second year of our marriage hardly a week went by when I didn't hear about how selfish I was being, refusing to grant Sally and her mother the help and support they needed. And also about how I was wasting my life, by the way. I still can't understand what all the fuss was about. I'm sure that Sally understood what an idiot I was when it came to business, and Bytemp came complete with a highly skilled staff of professionals when Wanda Temple took over.

I couldn't help thinking that Sally and Wanda just wanted me where they could keep their eyes on me.

Meanwhile Diamond Investigation was doing well enough to justify its existence, at least in my eyes. I had hired Darlene Roman to run the office and Darlene single-handedly took care of the business end, allowing me to remain a financial imbecile and concentrate on investigations.

Sally's attitude toward Darlene ran from chilly to glacial. Darlene was helping to keep the business going, which was at cross-purposes with Sally's plans.

And Darlene Roman looked very good in a skirt as well, though I never really suspected that Sally could be jealous.

Sally wanted me to give something up for her, and Diamond Investigation was all I had to sacrifice. I needed to feel that I had accomplished something on my own, and Diamond Investigation was all I had that qualified. Sally was a little selfish and insecure; I was insecure and a little lazy.

Of course, this is only Monday morning quarterbacking. I could be wrong.

Regardless, I could have tried a lot harder to save the marriage.

We both could have.

And Grace Shipley really had little to do with it.

TWELVE

"What are you doing here, Jake?" Sally asked, sitting across from me at a table in the hospital cafeteria.

Sally French was really very beautiful.

"I came to talk with Dick Spencer," I said.

"Richard is in no condition to talk right now."

"I guess he let it go a little too far before he spilled the beans to Crazy Al Pazzo."

I regretted saying it the moment it slipped out.

"He never told Pazzo a thing, Jake."

There's nothing like instant verification that you're being a jerk.

And nothing like hearing from your ex-wife that her new fiancé is much nobler than you are.

"Sorry," I said. "I heard that you and Richard were getting hitched. I guess it shocked me some. Congratulations."

I could tell by the way she looked at me

that she had no difficulty identifying a lame remark when she heard one.

"I'd really rather that you didn't bother Richard," she said. "He doesn't need any more trouble."

"I'm just trying to find out what happened with Jimmy. I would think that you'd be interested also."

"I'm not losing sleep over it. I cared for Jimmy; you know that. And I'm not saying that he deserved to die. But he did have a habit of flirting with trouble. And in any case, Richard has no ideas about what happened with Jimmy, as I'm sure he has already told you."

"I was hoping that Dick could help me understand all of the business angles."

"What do you want to know? Or did you forget that I have a master's degree in business administration?"

No, Sally, I didn't forget.

"Why do you think that Jimmy was hesitant to sell the Internet company? Half of a million bucks is a lot of money."

"A million can be chicken feed in the Internet business," she said.

And then she began to explain initial public offerings to a moron.

"I'll use round numbers to make it easier to compute. I'll assume that you know the difference between a privately owned company and a publicly owned company."

"Thanks for the vote of confidence."

"Do you want to hear this or not, Jake?"

"Sure, go ahead."

"Suppose that the owners of the company decided to go public with the business. An underwriter would have to be found and the number of shares to be offered would be determined. For the purpose of discussion, let's say it was a million shares. The underwriter would offer a number of those shares, let's say two hundred thousand, to inside investors, including the owners of the company, at a real value price before they went on the open exchange. Maybe five dollars a share, if someone thought that the company was worth paying a million dollars for. With me so far?"

"Right there," I said.

"The initial public offering, or IPO, would go on the exchange at a price also determined by the underwriter, say ten dollars a share. If enough interest is generated, as has been the case with many Internet IPOs, the stock could close as high as twenty dollars a share at the end of the first day of trading. Jimmy's shares would be worth four times what he paid for them. If Jimmy grabbed a hundred thousand shares, that's two million. A lot more than he could make selling outright to Richman."

"Where would Jimmy get five hundred grand to buy in?"

"He had his half of the company as collateral."

"What if the stock closed down from its initial offering price?"

"It's always a gamble, but as long as it stayed above five a share, Jimmy would be covered. The track record of Internet IPOs made it a pretty good bet."

"Why didn't you and Wanda go public with your company, Bytemp, if it's such a sure thing?" I asked.

I expected her to tell me that it was none of my business. She came very close to doing just that.

"I didn't say it was a sure thing; I said it was a good bet," she finally said, and added, "and who says we didn't?"

I could never be accused of missing a chance to push it.

"How'd you do?"

"Not bad, but you're getting off the subject."

OK.

"Do you think that Jimmy was aware of the potential?"

"Just because Jimmy was colorful didn't

make him stupid. Jimmy came to me not long ago and I ran him through it."

"So he wanted to go public with the company?"

"I don't know what he finally decided. You'll have to speak to the person he went to about trying to find an interested underwriter."

"And who would that have been, if I could ask?"

I was beginning to go timid on her.

"His old college buddy. You remember Linc, don't you, Jake?" she said.

Sure I remembered Linc, Lincoln French, the man who walked Sally down the aisle to meet me at the altar.

"Do you think your father would be willing to talk with me?"

"I have no clue. You're not his favorite person."

"Could you put in a good word for me?"

"Why would I want to do that, even if I could come up with a good word for you?"

"To help me find out who killed our friend Jimmy Pigeon?"

"Will you leave Richard alone if I help you?"

"Sure."

"I'll call my father, but I can't promise that he'll go for it."

"Good enough. I appreciate it, Sally."

"Stay away from Richard," she said.

She quickly rose from the table and walked away.

I let her leave without a word.

Again.

I turned my attention back to less complicated issues.

If there was so much potential profit in going public with Ex-Con.com, why would Harry Harding be inclined to sell out to Walter Richman for a measly million? I could only hope that Lincoln French would be willing to let ex-son-in-law bygones be bygones and tell me how he had advised Jimmy Pigeon. Since French was up in Sausalito it was time to get back up to the Bay Area. Any reason for getting out of LA was at least something.

With Dick Spencer in the hospital it looked like Vinnie would have to wait for his five grand, so I decided I'd take Boyle's advice and offer Strings a ride back with me.

I only wished I could say that I was looking forward to the company.

Tina Bella's payday would have to wait also, and the longer I had to keep her out of sight the better the chances that Crazy Al Pazzo's vast unintelligence network would succeed in locating her and punishing me.

Not a happy thought.

And Sally hadn't given me the chance to wake Spencer up and pull the name of Jimmy's ex-wife out of him. I was hoping to convince Spencer that Jimmy Pigeon would have wanted me to know, in case the woman was in any danger.

I wanted to convince myself.

When I turned the corner onto Bobby's street the first thing I saw was the black Cadillac sitting in front of the house and the very hefty Italian-American leaning on the front fender. I would have driven right by, but why get smart now? I pulled in behind the Caddy and got out of my car. Without ceremony the ape opened the back door of the Cadillac and motioned for me to get in.

I got in.

"Mr. Diamond, do you know who I am?" asked Crazy Al Pazzo.

Yeah, my worst nightmare.

"Yes, I do, Mr. Pazzo," I said. "I've seen you many times on television."

"I'm looking for Tina."

"Tina?" What the hell, might as well try.

"My wife, Tina Bella Pazzo."

"Oh, that Tina. I didn't know you two were married. Congratulations."

He gave me a look that could freeze baked ziti.

"Can you help me?" he asked.

"I'd love to help you, Mr. Pazzo, but I have no idea where Mrs. Pazzo might be."

I had decided to stop pushing my luck and go the respect route.

"You're fairly certain?"

Seemed like Alfonzo had been brushing up on his English. I resisted the impulse to say, "Quite certain."

"Yes, sir."

"In that case, I would like to employ your services."

Great.

"I'd love to help you, Mr. Pazzo," I said, "but I have pressing business in San Francisco and need to get back there right away."

"Perfect. I have reason to believe that my wife is somewhere in San Francisco. I'd like to hire you to find her."

Perfect.

"Mr. Pazzo, with all respect, I'm pretty bogged down with work at the present time. When it rains it pours; know what I mean?"

"Are you refusing to assist me, Mr. Diamond?"

Whatever gave him that idea? I wanted to say, "Don't be silly," but thought better of it. If I turned him down, my name would be put on a list that names didn't stay on for very long before they were scratched out permanently. And if it wasn't me it would be someone else hired to find Tina, so maybe this was a blessing in disguise.

Yeah, sure.

"I'd love to help you, Mr. Pazzo," I said, for the third time. "What makes you think that your wife has gone to San Francisco?"

"I have my ways," he said.

I bet he did.

"I'll give you four days to find her," he added.

"I don't work that way, Mr. Pazzo," I said, "sir."

"There's always a first time."

"I'll do my best."

"You do that," he said, and then after an interminable silence added, "you can get out of the car now, Mr. Diamond."

I got out of the car.

Al's gorilla got behind the wheel and the Caddy pulled away.

I was left to decide whether to return Bobby's tie or hang myself with it.

When I got into the house I called Willie Dogtail. I asked him to tell Vinnie to get ready to leave as soon as he returned from the racetrack. Vinnie was going to be a real pain in the ass for seven or eight hours in the car, complaining about having to go back without his five grand.

The phone rang the moment I placed the receiver in its cradle.

"Jake, two really big men barged in here about two hours ago all hot to speak with you. When I told them that you weren't here they insisted that I tell them where you lived."

"Slow down, Darlene."

I could hear her take a deep breath.

"Since Tina is at your place I thought it would be best to tell them you were down in LA, and when I understood they weren't particularly satisfied I thought I'd better tell them where in LA. I've been trying to warn you."

"It's OK, Darlene. You did the right thing. We've just been hired to find Tina Bella."

"By Crazy Al?"

"None other."

"Jesus, Jake."

"Is luck my middle name or what?"

"What are you going to do?"

Good question.

"I'm not sure, but at least he's giving me four days."

"What can I do?"

"Just stay calm, Darlene. I'll be back tonight. Why don't you go home in case they decide to revisit the office."

"You'll call me as soon as you get in?"

"I will."

"Be careful, Jake," she said.

"It may be a little too late for that. Go home."

I called the hospital. I had promised Sally that I wouldn't bother Spencer, but I thought that maybe I could urge him to send Tina's check up to San Francisco so that I could cut her loose. Of course Sally answered the phone in the hospital room.

"You promised not to bother him, Jake."

"Please, just ask him to send Tina Pazzo's money up to me as soon as possible. Tell him that the longer she has to wait the more danger she's in."

"I'll tell him. Good-bye."

"Thank you, Sally," I said, and then because nothing is ever enough with me I added, "Did you have a chance to speak with Lincoln?"

"I said I'd do it. I'm a little busy right now. I'll call him in the morning. Good-bye." The line went dead.

Nice going, Jake, I thought. Me, me, me.

I replaced Bobby's tie in his closet and wrote a short note thanking him for letting me use his place. I collected my few things, including what was left of the bottle of Dickel, and headed out to the street.

I checked the oil in the Chevy and topped it off with a quart from the trunk. I started the car and headed out to Santa Monica to pick up Vinnie at Dogtail's beach house.

I had wanted to make at least one more stop before leaving Los Angeles. I had planned to visit the office of Ex-Con.com, where Jimmy was killed, to see if Pigeon had left anything for me to go on.

I decided that it would have to wait.

Getting Vinnie out of town and figuring out what to do about Tina Pazzo were more immediate concerns. I could try to see Lincoln French and come back down if I thought it was necessary.

The drive up to San Francisco was just as I had imagined it would be, only worse. I couldn't shut Strings up about his money.

I finally managed to tune Vinnie out completely by going over all of the progress I had made by visiting Los Angeles.

It didn't take very long.

I had found Harry Harding. Maybe I had learned why Jimmy was reluctant to sell the company, but I still didn't know why Harding was hot to sell or where his widow stood on the question. I had learned that Jimmy Pigeon had an ex-wife but had no idea who she was or where she was or if she was in jeopardy. I had been very neatly assured by Ted Alster that Richman International was effectively out of the equation. I had agreed to hide Tina Bella, putting Darlene and myself in danger for the effort, and then I had been hired by Crazy Al Pazzo to find Tina.

Add it all up and it still totaled zero.

I tried my best to remain positive and optimistic.

Maybe Lincoln French could offer some insights on the sellout versus IPO debate. Maybe Dick Spencer would send Tina's check up right away. Maybe someone would come forward and confess to the murder of Jimmy Pigeon. Maybe Vinnie Strings would shut the fuck up already about his five thousand dollars.

"Vinnie, would you shut the fuck up already about the money? You'll get it when you get it."

Even I could be a brilliant analyst at times.

"I still can't believe that he left more to Tina than to you or me."

"I'm guessing she contributed more to his quality of life than we did, Vinnie."

It was almost midnight when I dropped Vinnie in front of his apartment house on Haight Street.

I drove over to return the Impala to Joey

Russo's garage. I climbed into the Toyota and headed over to my apartment in the Fillmore.

My two rooms looking out on Alamo Square were a far cry from the house that Sally and I had shared near the Presidio, but it felt good to be getting home.

At least that's what I thought until I got there.

The door to my apartment had been busted in, leaving a good part of the door frame attached to the door itself.

Tina Bella Pazzo was nowhere to be found.

THIRTEEN

The apartment looked as if a cyclone had run through it. Then again, that was pretty much the way I'd left it, so all that really told me was that Tina didn't have the time or inclination to straighten the place up while she was here.

I was almost too tired to be concerned about Tina. I didn't know if she had been here or not when the door was trashed. If it was one of Crazy Al's goons who had made firewood of the door frame, Tina could be on her way to somewhere she didn't want to be.

But I didn't think that her life was in danger.

The more pressing issue was the door itself. Since the landlord lived in Seattle and the super was usually too drunk to locate his own door, let alone mine, it would be a while before the thing was fixed unless I took care of it myself. Fortunately, I had some cash, a retainer from Pazzo, so I pushed a table against the door to hold it closed and planned to see to it in the morning.

What I needed more than anything was some shut-eye.

I had promised Darlene that I would call when I got in, and even though it was pretty late I thought I'd better do it or I'd hear about it later. She picked up after the first ring, so she either grabbed it in the middle of deep sleep or was sitting on the call.

"I made it back, Darlene. Sorry if I woke you."

"Jake, Tina just called. She's out in the street and doesn't know what to do. I would have told her to come here, but I knew it would piss you off."

"You're right. What happened?"

"She said she went out for a pack of cigarettes and got back just in time to see your door get demolished, so she beat it."

"Terrific. Where is she?"

"She's in a bar on the corner of Haight and Ashbury. Why don't you pick her up and you can both come over here?"

"Thanks, but I think we'll stay away from your place. I wouldn't want your boyfriend to get the wrong idea."

Darlene's boyfriend was a defensive

lineman for the 49ers.

"He's out of town."

"That's OK. I'll bring her over to Vinnie's."

"Bet you're looking forward to seeing Vinnie again after eight hours in the car with him."

"Can't wait."

"Do you think they'll come back, Jake?"

"I don't know, Darlene. I'm too tired to think straight. I'll drop Tina off with Vinnie and get a hotel room. In the morning I'll get my door fixed. Stay away from the office; I'll call you at home in the a.m."

"Don't call too early, Jake. It's Sunday around here."

"Great. It ought to be fun trying to find someone to fix the door on a Sunday morning."

"Joey Russo should be able to send someone over."

"Good idea. How'd you get to be so smart?"

"I'm only this smart when I'm half-asleep. Can I hang up now?"

"Go right ahead," I said. And she did.

I emptied the dirty clothes from my travel bag and threw in some less dirty ones. I collected Tina's things while I was at it. I stepped into the hall and used one of my stained neckties to pull the table up against the inside of the door as close as I could manage, which left it slightly ajar.

A shattered jar.

I got into the Toyota and headed up Haight Street toward the bar. I found Tina sitting in a booth toward the back, nursing a Manhattan.

"Was it Al's guys?" I asked, sitting down across from her.

"I don't know. It was one guy, and he didn't quite fit the bill. Too trim."

"I have your things in the car. I'll drop you over at Vinnie Strings' place until we can figure something out."

"I take it you don't have my check."

"Dick's having a hard time holding a pen right now."

"Vinnie's not going to hit on me, is he?"

"I doubt it. He resents you too much for beating him out in the inheritance sweepstakes."

"Are you staying at Vinnie's, too?"

"No, I'll grab a hotel room."

"Why don't you take me with you?"

"Not a good idea, Tina. I don't think Crazy Al would appreciate me shacking up with you in a hotel with money that he gave me to find you."

"Al hired you to find me?"

"The sweetheart gave me four days."

"So why would he send someone to your place?"

"Maybe he's hedging his bets."

"Maybe Al didn't send him."

"Come again?"

"Maybe the guy was looking for you. Maybe it has something to do with you snooping into Jimmy's death. But either way, what are you going to do about Al?"

"I'm going to pray that in four days I have no idea where you are."

"You want a drink?" she asked.

"No. Why don't you finish that one so we can get out of here."

While she was doing that I called Vinnie and told him I was on my way to drop Tina off. I told him I would get her out of there as soon as possible and that he should lay off her in the meantime.

After I left Tina with Vinnie I headed over to North Beach and checked into a small hotel in Little Italy. I used cash and checked in as Jacob Falco. I wish I could have believed that it would have made my grandfather proud. I asked the kid at the desk to give me a wake-up call at nine. It was already past two in the morning, and after all, it was Sunday.

I lay down in the bed, but I couldn't fall

asleep. As physically worn out as I was, my mind was doing calisthenics. I still had what was left of the Dickel in my bag. I passed on the cellophane-wrapped plastic cup and took a few pulls straight from the bottle, hoping it would help me get to sleep. I thought about Sally, how in spite of the jerk I could be she was still a good sport. I thought about what Tina had said, the suggestion that the door breaker may have been after me. If anyone thought I had learned anything of value in LA, they were dreaming. And Grace came to mind. How long had she been in Los Angeles and where had she gone off to just before Jimmy was killed?

Finally the booze did the job, but not without a price.

I dreamed that I had watched a carriage pull up to the front entrance of a countryside inn, somewhere along the road between Versailles and Paris.

Lucie Manette stepped out of the coach and entered the hostel, the coachman carrying her bags behind her. She looked a lot like Grace Shipley.

The driver returned, climbed to his position at the reins, and spurred the horses.

A passenger leaned forward in his seat to peer out of the coach window, and he stared at the door of the inn as the horses pulled away.

I couldn't make out the man's face.

SAVING GRACE

The trouble with you, Jacob,
is that you never seem to know what
the trouble is.

— GRACE SHIPLEY

FOURTEEN

I met Grace Shipley on the evening of the second anniversary of my marriage to Sally French.

During those first two years, Sally's desire to see me join the Bytemp team had moved from mild proposal, to strong recommendation, to relentless pressure. And Sally had a strong ally in her newly found mother, Mrs. Temple. They ganged up on me, and I was taking it personally.

To Sally's credit, she never exactly used the words *If you really loved me you would quit your ridiculous investigation business and help us run the company.*

She did, however, reach the point of suggesting that it was time that I decided what I wanted to be when I grew up.

When the anniversary day arrived we had been honoring a truce for almost a week in preparation for the historic occasion. We had planned to dine at the small French restaurant where we had gone on our first date, the idea being to create, or at least manufacture, a semblance of romance. We almost got away with it. But just before I left the office to meet Sally, I called home to tell her I was on my way.

"I'm heading out the door," I said. "I'll be there in twenty minutes."

"Great," Sally said. "It'll give us time for a drink before dinner. I bought some champagne."

"I can't wait. I'm feeling good, Sally, happy that we're going out tonight. How about you?"

"Me, too. Of course I could be *really* happy if you would change your mind about coming to work with us, Jake."

"Well, I hate to be the one to come between you and *real* happiness, but it just isn't going to happen!" I yelled.

And then I slammed down the telephone.

I don't know why I reacted so violently, and two seconds later I was sorry I had.

Sally shouldn't have said it. That was one night she could have let it rest.

But I could have brushed it off.

I suppose I was in no mood to restate for the hundredth time that I liked what I did for a living and had absolutely no interest in the importing and exporting of third-rate sporting equipment. It infuriated me that Sally couldn't let the day go by without making me have to say it again. The PI business had been slow at the time; Sally was carrying us and reminding me of the fact a little too often. Maybe it hurt my pride.

In any event, I failed to hold my tongue, and when I called back a few minutes later Sally didn't answer the telephone.

I needed a drink, so I naturally walked down to Little Mike's, just a block from my office on Columbus Avenue.

I decided I would try Sally again from the restaurant.

Little Mike's is where you went if you liked sitting at a bar, which I did. There you could watch Mike Crimi sauté your shrimp and garlic at the stove directly behind the bar, the flames jumping out of the frying pan as you sipped your bourbon.

Little Mike's is also where you went if you didn't want to be bothered, which I didn't. Unless someone like Grace Shipley ducks into the joint.

Then, if you're Jake Diamond and you had just hung up on your wife on your wedding anniversary, you find yourself being bothered a lot.

And not minding it all that much.

As I said, Grace *ducked* into Little Mike's.

She did all the classic moves. She came into the place backward. Once inside, she pressed herself up against the inside of the door, pushed it shut with her back, and closed her eyes as if it would make her invisible. It didn't work; every eye in Little Mike's was on her.

She stood there, holding her breath, and we all waited to see who was going to follow her in. Then someone pushed in from the outside.

She let out a gasp and let the door move her with it. Since her eyes were still closed, she couldn't see that it was only Georgio, Mike's delivery boy. When Georgio apologized for shoving her she opened her eyes, looked at the kid, and fainted.

Mike ran around from behind the bar, I went over from my barstool, and together he and I lifted her from the floor and moved her into the small back office and placed her onto the sofa.

I thought about waking her, but she looked so tranquil that I let her be. I sat at the desk and stared at her. Mike brought in my glass of bourbon and a pitcher of water. No one had come into the restaurant looking for her. I worked on the drink, and in a few minutes she opened her eyes and gazed into mine with a look that melted the ice in my George Dickel.

"Where am I?"

"In Little Mike's office, back of the restaurant you ducked into," I said. "So who are you trying to avoid?"

"Can I have some of that water?"

I poured a glass of the iced water and carried it over to her. She sat up on the couch, took the glass, and emptied it in one drink.

"Anyone follow me in?" she asked.

"Well, there was the delivery kid. You gave him quite a scare."

"I mean anyone looking for me?"

"Like who, for instance?"

"Like anyone."

"No."

"Do you have a name?" she asked.

"Jake. Jake Diamond. How about you?"

"Grace."

It figured.

"Can I trust you, Jake Diamond?" she asked.

In retrospect I should have said no.

"It's worth a try."

"I need a place where I can hide out, maybe for a day or two, just until I figure out what to do."

"Figure out what to do about what?" I asked.

"Could we forgo the specifics for the moment?"

"I like to know what I'm getting myself into."

It's a little idiosyncrasy of mine.

"I'll make you a deal," she said.

"I'm listening."

"You hide me out for a day or two and I'll tell you whatever you think you need to know to satisfy your curiosity. And I'll give you five hundred dollars."

"What makes you think that my services are for sale?"

"I'm sorry. I didn't mean to offend you," she said, with a smile that negated any iota of common sense I might still have had a loose grip on.

So instead of taking offense, I took the bait.

I certainly couldn't take her home with me to meet the wife.

I wasn't feeling too at ease about going home myself, at least until I could reach Sally on the phone and try to patch things up somehow. I knew that trying to call Sally was precisely what I should have been doing that very moment, instead of getting myself into something that I knew nothing about.

But why let what I knew get in my way.

In those days I was short of connections in San Francisco. When I wasn't in the office or out on a job Sally kept me on a pretty

142

short leash. It was before Vinnie Strings started hanging around and before I was at ease about calling on Joey Russo.

My two closest friends were Jimmy Pigeon and Sam Chambers, but Jimmy was in Santa Monica and Sam was doing time down in Obispo. Like it or not, I was going to have to involve Darlene. I called her at home from Mike's office.

"Hi, Jake. Happy Anniversary."

"Thanks. I need some help."

"If you're calling for advice, a dozen long-stemmed red roses, a bottle of really good champagne, and a couple of candles can't fail."

"I have a friend needs a place to lay low for a day or two. Can you put her up?"

"Jake, snap out of it; I'm almost out the door to the airport. I know you never listen to me, but I'm shocked that you forgot that I'm on vacation this week. Especially since you complained so much about having to make the coffee all by yourself."

"Jesus, I wasn't thinking."

"Try not making a habit of it. There's a spare set of keys in my desk at the office; she can stay here at my place while I'm gone if that suits her, as long as her wild parties don't include fraternity brothers. Who is she?"

"Just someone who dropped into Little Mike's in a jam."

"You took Sally to Little Mike's for your anniversary? How romantic."

"Romantic wasn't in the cards tonight. It's a long story. Yeah, sure, your place would be great."

"OK, take the keys. I don't have time for long stories. I'll be back in a week; try to stay out of trouble."

"Fat chance. Thanks, Darlene. I appreciate it."

"Time will tell," she said, and hung up the phone.

I turned to Grace. She had been acting tough, but I could see that she was very scared of something.

It only served to make her less resistible.

I decided to take her over to my office to pick up Darlene's house keys.

When we arrived at the door to my office, Grace read the printing on the opaque glass window.

" 'Diamond Investigation,' " she said as we walked in. "How about that."

I found Darlene's keys in her desk and snatched them up. I asked Grace to excuse me and went to my room in back to call Sally. I dialed the house with every intention of apologizing to Sally and begging her to meet me at the restaurant to try rescuing the anniversary plans. There was no answer.

I grabbed the bottle of bourbon and the two small glasses I kept on hand in my desk and went back out front.

"You know something?" she said as I handed her a glass. "I could really use a private investigator."

Before I could respond, Sally walked through the door.

"Working overtime, Jake?" she said, taking Grace in from head to toe.

"Sally, I just tried calling you. I can explain this."

"Save your breath," she said, and walked out.

"Sorry," said Grace. "I seem to have landed you in trouble."

"Don't worry; I think I can take full credit for this landing."

"What now? Are you going home tonight?"

"That's questionable. I'll take you over to Darlene's, and you can tell me what kind of work you had in mind for me if you're still interested in using me."

"If Darlene has a couch, you're welcome to stay," she said, smiling.

I was at a loss for a comeback.

I drained the bourbon from my glass and

led her out of the office. We climbed into the Toyota and drove in silence.

"I really would like to employ your services," she finally said, "and if you're up for it you could start right now."

"What did you have in mind?"

"Could we make a stop on the way? I need some things to wear."

I glanced at my Timex. It was well after ten.

"Unless you do your clothes shopping at 7-Eleven, it's a little late."

"I have clothing; we just need to pick it up where I left it."

"Expecting someone to be waiting for you there?"

"I don't think so. I have a suitcase in a locker at Union Station."

To play it safe, I left Grace in the car and went in myself to pick up her things. I threw the suitcase into the backseat and drove. I was trying my best to avoid thinking about what I was getting myself into.

When we reached Darlene's, Grace made herself right at home. She kicked off her shoes, started some coffee, and asked if it would be OK if she took a quick shower. I told her that when Darlene offered a place to stay, the shower was thrown in. I sat at the kitchen table, feeling uneasy, and decided to call Sally. There was no answer at home.

Grace walked into the kitchen wearing a white terry cloth robe, poured two cups of coffee, and sat down.

"Are you going home?" she asked.

"I don't think so."

"I'm glad. I really don't want to be alone."

"I need to know who you're running from," I said.

"The police," she answered. "They think I killed my husband."

"Someone killed your husband?"

"I don't think so. It's just that no one seems to be able to find him and the police think that I had the motive and opportunity to make him disappear."

"The motive being money?"

"Physical abuse."

If her husband had beat up on her, he had stayed away from her face.

"And the opportunity?"

"I was the last person known to have seen him, alive or otherwise."

"Which was when?"

"Two weeks ago."

"Where?"

"At home."

"So what happened?"

"He tried to roundhouse me, I ducked, and he punched the wall. His hand was dripping blood like a faucet and he was chasing me all over the house. Finally I locked myself in the bathroom, and when I came out he was gone."

"You called the cops?"

"The police just showed up. The neighbors must have complained about the commotion. They found all that blood and no body, so they took me in for questioning. One of the lady officers uncovered more than a few bruises on my arms and torso, and they decided to hold me. A friend got me out on bail, but this morning the police showed up again. I went out the back door with a suitcase, thought of hopping a train but didn't know where to go. I left my things in the locker at the train station and roamed around Fisherman's Wharf until I saw a patrol car and panicked."

She paused to take a drink of coffee.

"I ducked into the restaurant, and you know the rest."

"And you think that your husband is alive somewhere?"

"Yes. I doubt he bled to death from a cut on his hand. But if I don't locate him I'm screwed; pardon my language," she said. "Funny, I never thought I'd ever want to find the bastard."

"So you want me to help you find your

husband, at least prove that he's not a corpse."

"That's the general idea, yes."

"Any clue where to start?"

"No. I gave every idea I had to the police, and they couldn't track him down. His friends, his family, people at his job, the guys at his tennis club, no one's heard a word. It's like he dropped off the face of the earth."

"It would be nice to have somewhere to begin," I said.

"His name is Frank Slater, if that's any help."

"Frank Slater the attorney?"

"That's him."

It happened to be a great help. Not only did I know of Frank Slater, the *mob* lawyer; I also knew someone who could possibly lead me right to him. The question was, did I want to go there.

At that time I didn't know Joey Russo all that well.

I had yielded to his insistence that I garage my Chevy at his place, but his world seemed a little too scary to me.

Something about Grace Shipley inspired me to throw all caution to the wind. I've always been a sucker for a damsel in distress.

I should have been thinking more about

the one I had married.

I told Grace she should get some sleep, assuring her she was safe there at Darlene's and that I had a plan. I told her that I would get right to it in the morning.

I actually did use the couch that night.

I tried calling Sally a few more times before I finally fell asleep but got no answer. It was unlikely that Sally would have been out all night, unless she went to her mother's. I figured she was just ignoring the phone or had unplugged the thing.

The next morning I left Grace asleep and headed over to my office. I wasn't looking forward to having to make the coffee myself. It was the same coffee, the same coffeemaker, and the same water, but it was always better when Darlene made it.

There was a message on the answering machine from a lawyer named Spencer asking that I call. I put it on the bottom of my list.

I called Joey Russo and ran the story by him and asked if he could help me locate Frank Slater. I told Joey that I was getting paid to find Slater and he would be compensated for the help he gave me. He told me not to be insulting. He said he would get back to me.

I tried Sally again at home, no answer. I

tried her mother's, no answer. I tried her office at Bytemp and was told that she wasn't in. I asked for Mrs. Temple and was told that she wasn't in. I'm no rocket scientist, but I had the feeling that I was being avoided.

I was just about to call the number that Spencer had left on my machine when the phone rang.

"Mr. Diamond, my name is Richard Spencer. I'm an attorney retained by your wife to initiate divorce proceedings."

"Are you sure you have the right Mr. Diamond?" I asked.

"Positive," he answered.

"Don't be ridiculous," I said.

"I assure you, Mr. Diamond, that is definitely not my intention. You will soon be receiving papers in the mail. Meanwhile Ms. French has requested that you not try to contact her directly but instead conduct all communication with her through my office."

For lack of a better term, I was flabbergasted.

"Where is she? I want to talk with her."

"I can see why one of her complaints was that you don't listen. I'll quickly rephrase it for you, and then I really must be getting back to work."

"I heard you, asshole," I said, and slammed down the receiver.

I truly never saw it coming. Sure, Sally and I had our differences of opinion, particularly about my day job. But I had no idea she was so close to the edge that my actions the night before would push her over.

And now I was angry.

And that wouldn't help me to deal with Grace Shipley.

There's nothing like lack of trust to encourage untrustworthiness.

I tried to distract myself and cool down by piddling with the papers that Darlene had left on my desk. A few bills for our services, which she wanted me to look over before mailing. A few messages requiring return calls. A copy of the bank statement for the business, which didn't cheer me up much. The phone number where Darlene would be staying, in case I couldn't find the start button on the coffee machine. That little note did get a smile out of me.

I made a few phone calls. One was to a woman who thought that her husband was having an affair and wanted to find out if it was true. I really wasn't in the mood. I told her that she might be better off not knowing, but if she decided to go ahead I could see her the following afternoon.

Nine times out of ten they didn't call back.

Then I called Jimmy Pigeon down in LA. He had left a message with Darlene, said it wasn't important, just checking in.

"Hey, Jimmy, I heard you called."

"Nothing urgent, Jake. Just wanted to see how you and Sally were doing and wish you a Happy Anniversary."

I wish now that I had opened up to Jimmy about the situation with Sally and had mentioned my run-in with Grace Shipley.

Things might have turned out very differently.

Instead I just said "thanks" and "we're doing fine" and "how are you?" Jimmy and I promised each other that we would make it our business to get together sometime soon, and that was it.

And then I decided that I didn't want to be there alone in the office anymore, so I put the call forwarding over to Darlene's home number and went back to see how Grace was doing.

A lot more vulnerable than when I'd left.

I stopped on the way to pick up a bottle of bourbon and made another detour at the supermarket. I didn't know what Grace's eating habits were, but there wasn't much around Darlene's for someone who enjoyed more than twigs and leaves. It looked as if I might be camping out on the couch for a while, so I picked up some meat and potatoes. I thought it would be better to cook in and order in while the heat was on.

We made lunch and talked about the weather. I told her that I was waiting for possible word on Slater; I didn't mention my chat with Sally's lawyer. After a few hours Grace said she was feeling cooped up and asked if we could take a ride. I thought that a drive over to Berkeley wouldn't be too risky; we could walk around the university and envy the college kids. We spent the afternoon peering into store windows and strolling around the fountain on the UC campus.

We had dinner in Berkeley and took in a movie. Grace seemed much more relaxed. She had adopted a sense of security, hopefully not a false one.

For my part, I had distanced myself from the anger that I had felt after talking with Sally's mouthpiece.

Grace and I were helping each other to ignore reality.

It was late when we arrived back at Darlene's. Grace went into the bedroom to change into her sleep gear, and I opened the convertible sofa. I poured a tall glass of bourbon, knowing that I'd need some help falling asleep. Grace came in and asked if there was another glass around.

We sat on the couch, sipping our drinks, not saying much. One drink led to another; one thing led to another. I'll spare you the details, but when the phone rang at eight the next morning the sofa bed hadn't been slept in.

It was Joey Russo with the story on Frank Slater.

The critical news was that Slater was alive and the police weren't interested in Grace anymore.

Here were the specifics.

Frank Slater had been working as a lawyer for the Carlucci crime family for years, unbeknownst to his wife of six months. Shortly after he married Grace, Slater was picked up by the feds and told that if he didn't cooperate he would be spending his new bride's childbearing years in a federal penitentiary.

They had the goods on him.

The situation made him temperamental, and he began taking his frustrations out on his wife. Whoever he thought he was symbolically lashing out at, Grace became the unlucky object of his brutality.

On the night Slater smashed his hand into

the wall he was on his way to meet with Johnny Carlucci to discuss ways that John might beat a murder rap. Slater was wearing a recording device, compliments of the Justice Department. When the ruckus began between Slater and his wife, the agents at the other end of the wire rushed in.

They whisked Slater out of the house and tended to his damaged hand. He missed the meeting with Carlucci, which actually saved his life.

Carlucci had discovered that Slater was working with the Feds and was planning to knock the lawyer off at the meeting. A phone tap alerted the FBI to the planned hit. The government had no choice but to settle for Slater's testimony and rushed him and his freshly bandaged hand straight into the Witness Protection Program. The San Francisco police were out of the loop, so they were handling his disappearance as an incident of foul play and liking Grace as a suspect.

It had taken two weeks for the word to get to the SFPD that the whereabouts of Frank Slater were of no concern to them, and they were coming to tell Grace that she was cleared when she beat it out the back door.

That was the good news.

The bad news was that Grace could be in danger.

"Mrs. Slater could be in danger," said Russo.

"Why? She doesn't know anything," I insisted.

It's what I wanted to believe.

"I believe you, but what I believe doesn't much matter. Carlucci needs to be convinced that his business wasn't pillow talk. On top of that, Carlucci might be thinking that the wife can help him find out where the Feds stashed Slater."

"How would she know?"

"She wouldn't. But if Slater thought that his wife was in danger it might smoke him out."

"He couldn't care less about what happens to her. All she was to him was an ornament and a punching bag."

"Save your arguments for Johnny Boy."

"What do you mean?"

"The only way out of this is to set up a powwow between John Carlucci and the woman and persuade him that she's no threat and of no use," said Joey. "I can arrange it, and even sit in, but the verdict will be out of my hands."

"That's it?"

"Unless she wants to go to the FBI and ask them to make her disappear the same way they made Slater vanish."

"OK, thanks. I'll let you know."

"Don't wait too long," he said.

It didn't take long. I ran it by Grace and she insisted she wanted to meet with Carlucci. I called Joey back and asked him to set it up.

That night we sat around a table in Carlucci's North Beach restaurant. "Johnny Boy" Carlucci, Joey Russo, Grace Shipley Slater, and myself. It had been decided that Joey would do the talking, since he was best versed in the lingo. While Russo laid out the case for the defense, Carlucci never took his eyes off Grace.

When Joey had completed his closing statements, Carlucci asked to speak with the lady in private.

Two orangutans escorted Joey and me to the bar and plied us with drinks while Grace and Johnny talked. Twenty minutes later we were brought back to the table.

"So," asked Carlucci, "how about some dinner? The food is excellent."

I'm sure it was. His mother ran the kitchen.

"No thank you," said Joey. "We really should be going."

Carlucci rose from his seat and thanked us for coming. Joey Russo shook Carlucci's hand, and we walked out of the restaurant.

Joey drove us back to Darlene's. He talked about the Giants. He didn't say a thing about the meeting or ask Grace anything about her conversation with Carlucci. It was none of his business, and he showed me by example that it was none of mine.

So I never knew what Grace said to John Carlucci, but whatever it was, it did the trick. As far as I could see, Carlucci seemed to lose all interest in her.

While I was becoming more and more interested.

All of my attempts to contact Sally were in vain. Soon I gave up.

Everything went pretty quickly after that.

I began spending a lot of time with Grace.

Meanwhile the *Diamond versus Diamond* divorce proceedings were moving along, not rapidly but efficiently. And in Grace's case, the government was seeing to it that Slater sign all the necessary papers for a divorce and a liquidation of his assets. Eventually Grace would be at least financially compensated for the abuse she had taken from her ex-husband.

While we were waiting for the monetary affairs to be settled I gladly took the role of breadwinner. Grace moved out of the house she had shared with Slater and into my place on Fillmore Street.

Then, six months later, I was called down to Los Angeles to meet with Sally and her lawyer to finalize an uncontested divorce. Sally looked fantastic. After the meeting and paperwork, Sally and I decided to have dinner together. And then a few drinks after dinner.

Surprisingly, we got along pretty well.

It was a lot easier since we weren't obliged to.

After half a year we may have forgotten most of what had made us both so angry in the first place.

I wanted to tell Sally that it wasn't Grace who had come between us.

Explain that Grace happened later, after the space was already there.

I wanted to apologize to Sally for giving up so easily. Sally could have used an apology. Sally deserved one.

I could have forgotten for a moment that Sally had also given up without much fight and that I could have used an apology also.

I let the opportunity pass.

We grabbed a cab and I dropped Sally off at the apartment she kept in LA for business. I went back to my hotel. I had mixed emotions about the finality of the divorce. On the one hand, there was a sense of sadness and failure. On the other, it freed me to think more seriously about a future with Grace.

I flew back to San Francisco the next morning, eager to see her.

When Grace wasn't there to pick me up at the airport I was a little worried.

When I arrived back at the apartment Grace was gone.

Really gone.

Everything.

When the phone rang I leaped at it. I was certain that it was Grace with a good explanation.

It was an explanation, but it was Joey Russo on the telephone, and it wasn't good at all.

Joey had just learned it; I knew better than to ask him how.

The money that Grace had coming to her, from the sale of Frank Slater's house and his other assets, had been handed over to her by the Justice Department.

Nearly a week before.

Nearly two hundred thousand dollars.

Grace had patiently waited until I left for my meeting in Los Angeles.

She hadn't given me any clue. She had seemed genuinely disappointed that I would be spending the night in LA.

She took me to the airport and told me to hurry back.

And it was so long, Jake; it's been good to know you.

I hadn't heard anything from Grace or about Grace in nearly three years.

Not even a mention of her name until Evelyn Harding dropped it at my office four days earlier.

What puzzled me most was why Jimmy Pigeon had never mentioned her in all that time, not even in passing, no matter how much he thought it would upset me.

And why I had such a strong feeling that Jimmy was screaming Grace Shipley's name out to me now.

FIFTEEN

The bedside telephone woke me like a fire alarm. The fire was in my brain. I grabbed the receiver on the second ring, before it turned my head into kindling.

"Grace?" I said.

"Suzie, from the front desk. This is your nine a.m. wake-up call, Mr. Falco."

I placed the receiver down and popped upright in the bed. After a few seconds I remembered that I was in a hotel room and that I had an apartment door that needed repair.

I dialed Joey Russo's number.

"Jake, I heard you dropping off the Chevy last night. You should have stopped in for a drink."

"No offense, Joey. I was pretty beat. I need a favor."

"Whatever I can do."

"Know anyone who can fix a door for me on a Sunday?"

"Absolutely. When and where?"

"My place, as soon as possible."

"What happened?"

"Looked like someone used a battering ram in place of a key."

"Think they'll be back?"

"I'm not sure what to think."

"Want me to have someone keep an eye on your place for a while just in case?"

"That would be good, Joey, thanks a lot."

"I'll have him down there in an hour. His name is Sonny the Chin. He'll have your door back good as new in no time and then make sure that no one gets within ten feet of it without your permission."

"Great. Thanks, Joey."

"Anything else I can do?"

"Well, maybe."

"Don't be shy."

"I need to keep Tina Bella out of sight for a few days."

"As in Tina Bella Pazzo?"

"Yeah. Crazy Al is hunting for her and she'd rather not get bagged."

"You shouldn't be messing with Crazy Al. I, on the other hand, love messing with him. The greasy bastard gives Italian-American businessmen like myself a bad name. I'll take care of it; just tell me where to have her picked up. Let me know when you want her back; until then it's better you don't know where she is."

"I don't know how to thank you, Joey."

"Don't worry, Jake. We'll think of something."

I decided that it would be more economical to make the other calls from my apartment, so I checked out of the hotel. At the same time I didn't want to get home before Joey's man arrived, just in case anyone unfriendly was waiting for me.

I headed over to Darlene's place to kill some time. With any luck, Darlene would invite me to stay for breakfast.

When I pulled up in front of Darlene's house I realized that I should have phoned her first. It was still fairly early for a Sunday morning. She had asked me not to call too early, let alone show up unannounced. I was almost about to leave when she appeared at the car window running in place in a Reebok sports bra, Adidas shoes, and a pair of Nike shorts.

"Had breakfast yet?" she asked, a little out of breath but not looking bad for someone who had just run five or six miles.

"I could use a bite."

"You can start the bacon while I shower."

"I didn't know you ate bacon," I said, getting out of the car.

She trotted up to the front door.

"I don't. I keep it around for the boyfriend. Keeps his cholesterol level at the NFL minimum requirement."

I decided to pass on the bacon, so while Darlene showered I made a few phone calls instead.

I called Vinnie and told him to expect someone to take Tina off his hands. I told him to make sure that whoever showed up could prove that Joey Russo had sent him. I told Vinnie to stay away from my place and the office until he heard from me.

I phoned Lincoln French at his home in Marin County. Lincoln and his wife, Jenny, had adopted Sally the day she was born. Lincoln, who was semiretired, had made his mark as a stockbroker and investment counselor. Lincoln and Jenny were totally devoted to Sally, who had been their only child. Both parents had chosen to hold me responsible for the failure of the marriage.

Lincoln French and Jimmy Pigeon had met in college and had remained friends for nearly forty years. If Lincoln decided to help me, or agreed to talk with me at all for that matter, it would only be as a result of his affection for Jimmy.

After three rings, Jenny French picked up the phone.

"Hello, Jenny," I said, wishing her husband had answered. "How are you?"

"Hold on; I'll get Lincoln," was all she said.

"I can meet you at my office in Sausalito tomorrow morning at ten. I can give you thirty minutes," said Lincoln French.

"Thank you, Lincoln. I'll be there."

"I'm doing it for Jimmy. If you feel compelled to thank someone, thank Sally."

And that was it.

"I don't smell the bacon," said Darlene, coming into the kitchen in a white terry cloth robe, a towel wrapped around her head. She looked like Rita Hayworth.

"Didn't want to make you envious."

"Why don't you grab that melon off the top of the refrigerator and cut it up while I throw on an outfit? We can have it with some yogurt. If you have time, push the little red button and get the coffee going."

"I'll make time," I said.

Yogurt and fresh fruit. Yum.

I started the coffee and picked up the *Sunday Examiner.*

"How you coming on that cantaloupe?" asked Darlene, returning to the kitchen. I realized that it was still sitting on top of the refrigerator.

"I kind of lost my appetite."

"In case you change your mind," she said,

pouring the coffee, "there's a cherry cheese Danish ring in the fridge."

"More defensive lineman food?"

"Yes. I don't even like to look at it."

Fighting the urge to pounce on the Danish, I filled Darlene in while she worked on her low-fat organic yogurt.

"Wow, Jimmy had a wife. When did he touch base with her again?" she asked.

"I have no idea. Spencer wasn't talking."

"What was it like to see Sally?"

"I'm not sure."

"I bet you're looking forward to seeing her father."

"I always liked Lincoln French. I'm sure he's looking forward to the meeting less than I am. I have little left to go on besides the value of Jimmy's share of the company, so I guess I'll have to bother him."

"I see," she said.

I sensed that Darlene was preoccupied.

"Tell me, Darlene. Why do you think Jimmy never told me he kept in touch with Grace Shipley?"

"Knowing Jimmy, I'm sure that he was acting with your interests in mind. I hate to say it, Jake, but sometimes you need a little protection from yourself."

Darlene was never reluctant to say what she hated to say.

"Have any plans for today?" I asked, just to move past it.

"I have quite a few plans, and the day isn't getting any younger."

"Remind me to never bother you again on a Sunday morning, Darlene."

"C'mon, Jake; don't be so sensitive. I'm just playing with you. You can bother me anytime you like."

"Thanks."

"Besides, reminding you about anything is a waste of time."

"I'd better get going to my apartment. Check to see if Sonny the Chin made it over there yet."

"I'm not even going to ask," she said. "Would you please do me a big favor, Jake?"

"Anything at all, Darlene."

"Take the Danish ring with you."

When I reached my apartment, Sonny the Chin was almost done rebuilding the portion of the door frame that had been torn off when the door was kicked in.

"You work fast," I said, coming up behind him very quietly. He didn't even flinch.

"I would have had it done, but it took a while to calm him down."

Sonny pointed into the kitchen where a scrawny guy with a lopsided mustache was tied to one of the chairs.

"Where did he come from?" I asked.

"He was skulking around in the hallway when I showed up, so I kind of invited him in," Sonny said. "Is that a cherry cheese Danish ring?"

I handed him the box.

"What's the blue stuff over his mouth?"

"Masking tape. Works as well as duct tape but doesn't hurt as much when you tear it off."

"That's very considerate."

"You do what you can within the parameters," he said, and went back to work on the door.

I walked into the kitchen and looked at Sonny's catch. I pulled the tape off his mouth.

"Who sent you?" I asked, to the point if not original.

He began to insist that he was an innocent bystander and complain about the rough treatment Sonny had given him.

I put the tape back over his mouth.

"Sonny!" I called.

"Yes, Mr. Diamond?"

"Call me Jake. You think this is the guy who creamed the door last night?"

"I hope so," Sonny said.

"He's not cooperating. Have any ideas?"

"Well, if you're not as attached to that

170

chair as he is, we could toss them both out the window and be done with it."

The guy in the chair started mumbling. I removed the tape again.

"I don't know," he said.

"You don't know who sent you?"

"I get a call. I take an assignment. I get cash wired to me. I do what I'm paid to do and don't ask questions."

"Sonny?"

"I wouldn't be surprised, Jake; he looks like the type."

"How much did you get paid?" I asked, turning back to our guest.

"Two grand."

"To do what?"

"Break down the door. I wasn't going to hurt anyone; that's not part of the deal."

"So you did it. What brought you back?" I asked.

"The television. I wanted it last night, but I didn't have my car."

"You should be ashamed of yourself," I said. "Have any cash on you?"

"Inside jacket pocket, Jake," Sonny said. "His wallet claims he's Vic Stritch."

Sonny the Chin was a thorough guy.

I reached for Strich's wallet and pulled out ten one-hundred-dollar bills.

"Five should cover the door, Vic. The

other five I'll hold in escrow. You come up with a name on your client and you'll get it back. Now I'm going to untie you and you're going to disappear."

I untied him and followed him to the front door. Sonny and I watched him vanish.

"Any idea who sent him?" asked Sonny.

"Al Pazzo?"

"I don't think so. Using a fuckup like that guy Stritch is a little lacking in finesse," said Sonny, "even for Crazy Al. Pazzo is known for the more personal approach. And he uses only Italians."

"Well, that leaves me out of guesses," I said.

"Maybe you learned something in LA and you just don't know it yet."

"It wouldn't be the first time."

"I'm just thinking out loud," Sonny said. "Maybe someone hoped that dealing with carpentry issues would take your mind off the bigger picture."

"Interesting thought," I said, holding out five bills to him.

"It's covered," he said, "a favor for Mr. Russo. I should have this finished in less than an hour. If you're worried about intruders, Joey asked me to stick around."

"That's OK. Unless you think that Vic will be back."

"Not unless he brings some information that would inspire you to free his escrow account," Sonny said.

And then he went back to work on the door frame.

I called Vinnie Strings.

Vinnie told me that Joey Russo had just picked up Tina Bella and taken her to who knows where.

It was almost noon and I hadn't eaten a thing; having passed on the yogurt with Darlene. I had handed the cherry cheese ring to Sonny; I wasn't about to ask for it back. I decided that I had better get some food in me before I got to the point of being totally useless.

I was flattering myself in thinking that I hadn't reached that point already.

I told Sonny the Chin that I was taking off for a while. He handed me two keys that he said would open my new door lock. He said he would leave when he was done, but that I could call Joey Russo if I needed him for anything. I thanked him for his help and headed out.

I went over my to-do list as I drove over to the Mission. It was going pretty well, considering. The door was taken care of thanks to Joey Russo. Also thanks to Joey, Tina was safe for the time being. Hopefully I could get her money and send her off to points far south before Crazy Al's four-day grace period ran out. And I had set up an appointment with Lincoln French.

I slid into a booth in Pedro's Famous Burrito Palace at Fourteenth and Valencia. Whatever made me think I wanted Mexican food had already slipped my mind.

Pedro's daughter came over to take my order.

I went with the Chicken and Jalapèno Grande. Perhaps not the best way to break my fast, so I also ordered a shot of tequila and a Budweiser to alert the digestive system.

I wanted to talk with Grace Shipley, even if I didn't know exactly why.

Grace had left town before Jimmy was killed. I wanted to know if she had seen him while she was there. Evelyn could probably tell me where to find Grace, but I didn't think she would. I wondered if I could get it out of Harding's daughter.

I knocked down the shot of Cuervo Gold and sipped the Bud.

When the food came it snarled at me from the plate.

I used my fork to cut into what was a mean-looking chicken burrito. I could swear I heard it growl, *"Back off, gringo."*

Fifteen minutes later I was in the Toyota again. I had left most of the burrito sitting at the booth in Pedro's. My stomach was doing cartwheels and the Mylanta was in the glove box of the Chevy. I made a quick stop at a drugstore for two bottles, one for home and one for the office, and headed back to my apartment.

I threw down a long shot on my way up the stairs to my rooms.

Sonny had done a fine job, complete with a WET PAINT sign stuck on the door with blue masking tape. The new key opened the new lock and it seemed I was secure.

Sonny had left what remained of the Danish ring, but even though I was still hungry I resisted the temptation. I thought that it wouldn't hurt to lie down for a while. I hadn't slept very well; the bed at the hotel had been like an old sponge.

I pulled off my shoes and threw myself down on my Beauty Rest.

I went out like a light.

SIXTEEN

I was awakened by a furious pounding that rattled the small table at the side of the bed.

For a moment I thought it was an earthquake and would have crawled under the bed except for the fact that the box spring and mattress were on the floor. When I finally realized that the thumping was coming from my front door I jumped up off the bed and yelled something like *hold your horses.* The banging continued, and it was definitely putting Sonny the Chin's handiwork to the test.

On my way past the dresser I caught a glimpse of myself in the mirror and nearly screamed. I seriously considered stopping to do something about my hair but couldn't imagine what could be done with it. The racket was getting louder, it sounded as if there actually were a team of horses out there to hold onto, so I let go of my vanity and rushed to the door looking like Albert

Einstein's illegitimate son.

When I reached the door I opened it as quickly as possible, in a valiant attempt to rescue the fresh paint job. I nearly lost my teeth for the effort.

My visitor had reared back to give the door another massive blow and his fist was greeted by thin air, thin air located extremely close to my chin. The momentum carried him into the apartment and it was only my reading chair that stopped him from going through the rear window and into the Dumpster in the alley below. The collision with the chair upended him, and he landed on his back in the kitchen doorway. He looked up at me and suddenly the condition of my hair was of little concern. This guy had a face that looked like it had been run through a meat grinder.

"Jake Diamond?" he asked from the floor.

If I had ever wondered what Godzilla would have sounded like if he could speak, my curiosity was satisfied.

"Who wants to know?" I asked.

Hey, I just woke up.

"San Francisco police," was the answer.

It didn't come from the floor, it came from behind me, and it was a woman's voice.

"I'm Lieutenant Lopez and he's Sergeant

Johnson," she said. "So are you Jake Diamond or what?"

I turned around and all I could think of was Beauty and the Beast. She had sky blue eyes that made the sky look brown and a figure that made Demi Moore look like a boy. I wondered what time it was.

"What time is it?" I asked. "Do you have ID?"

"Nine thirty-seven," she said, flashing her badge while Johnson struggled to his feet. I couldn't believe that I had slept for nearly six hours.

"And the question was?"

"Are you Jake Diamond?"

"At your service," I said with a big smile that often worked but didn't go over with her at all. It might have been my hair.

"We have a female corpse downtown with a bullet hole in her forehead and she had this in her handbag," said Lopez, holding up an envelope that had miraculously appeared in her hand.

"What's that?" I asked.

"An envelope," said Lieutenant Lopez.

Give me a break.

"With your name and address all over it, Diamond," said Johnson, finally back in the game.

"You moonlighting at the post office?"

"Mr. Diamond," said the lieutenant, "there's no reason to be rude."

"There was no reason to try to pulverize my front door."

"We were concerned for your safety."

"This is the Fillmore, not Rockingham," I said. "Mind if I see the letter?"

"Sorry, it's evidence," said Lopez. "Aren't you just a little curious about who the victim is?"

Come to think of it I was, but then again I really didn't want to know.

"I don't know."

"Well, I'll tell you anyway, just in case it turns out you are. Her name was Christina Pazzo."

"That's impossible," I said. I was so sure that Tina would be absolutely safe under the protection of Joey Russo that I couldn't accept it.

"Everything in the woman's bag indicated that it's not impossible," said the lieutenant.

"Mind if I make a phone call?" I asked. I needed to get hold of Joey right away and find out if he'd lost Tina somehow.

"You bet, Diamond," Johnson piped in. "As soon as we get to the station you can call anyone you like."

"Am I under arrest?"

"Only if you'd like to be, Mr. Diamond.

Or you could just be coming in to answer a few routine questions," said Lopez.

Johnson and Lopez were kind enough to offer me a ride to Vallejo Street Station. Not that I had any choice. They did let me attempt to straighten out my hair, but it was basically a waste of time.

Neither detective said a word during the fourteen-minute drive. They were, no doubt, afraid that if they questioned me in the car the interrogation would be over before we got there. Which was true.

Instead I sat in silence, staring at the backs of their heads. Lopez's Breck Girl strawberry-blond hair and Johnson's lack of it.

Johnson was shaved bald with a nine-forty-five shadow. He had a long scar at the base of his cranium. The scar curved slightly upward at each end, and there were two large moles just above ear level, spaced approximately six inches apart. Poke a carrot stick in the middle and he'd look like a fuzzy Frosty the Snowman. It was a vast improvement over the front of his head.

When we reached the police station they placed me in an interview room for the mandatory twenty-minute wait. They were considerate enough to let me use the phone, so I called Joey.

"Russo residence, Joseph Russo Senior speaking."

Joey cracked me up sometimes.

"Joey, it's Jake. How's Tina doing?"

"Seemed fine last time I saw her."

Great.

"When and where was that, Joey?"

"Something wrong, Jake?"

"I'm not sure."

"I gave her a five grand advance on her inheritance and dropped her at the airport about three hours ago. She was in a real yank to get out of the country and she was getting on Angela's nerves."

Angela is Mrs. Joey Russo, and it didn't take much to aggravate her.

"That was good of you, Joey."

"So why does it sound like you're not real happy?"

"The cops have me down here at Vallejo Street. They have a dead body in the basement they seem to think is Tina."

"Jesus, Jake, did you see the body?"

"No."

"Do the cops think you did something?"

"I don't know what they think. They're making me wait the wait."

"I'll be right down," he said, and the line went dead.

Ten minutes later Lieutenant Lopez

walked into the room. Frosty wasn't in attendance.

"So, Mr. Diamond, where were you at around eight-thirty this evening?"

"In the middle of a bad dream. I should have thanked your partner for waking me. Has anyone identified the body?"

"Not yet. We're trying to locate her husband," Lopez said.

Bad idea.

"Mind if I take a look?"

"Are you admitting that you could identify Christina Pazzo?"

"Yes, I am. In fact, I saw her just last night, but if you tell Crazy Al that I said so I'll deny it."

"I'll be right back," Lopez promised.

Yeah, sure.

To my surprise, she was back in less than five minutes, Johnson in tow.

"Let's go," she said.

They led me down the hall and down the stairwell to the basement.

I'd been in the morgue more than once before, but it still gave me the creeps.

It has a smell all its own, as unpleasant as the smell it was trying to cover up.

I waited with Lopez while Johnson went to find the medical examiner to locate the body in question.

"What was your relationship to Mrs. Pazzo?" Lopez asked.

"No need to be jealous, Lieutenant, just friends."

She looked as if she was about to say something but decided not to. Instead she gave me another straight line.

"And what about you and Mr. Pazzo?"

"My relationship with Crazy Al Pazzo could be compared to the relationship between a wolf and a chicken, where I'm the chicken."

Johnson waved us over from across the room.

Johnson stood over a stainless-steel gurney; a white sheet was thrown over the shape of a human body. When we reached him, he slowly lifted the sheet away from the head of the corpse.

"Well, Mr. Diamond, can you identify her?" asked Lopez.

I looked down, unable to hide the surprise on my face.

"I can identify her," I said sadly, "but it's not Tina Bella Pazzo."

The lieutenant and the sergeant looked at each other and then at me.

"If it's not Mrs. Pazzo," said Lopez.

"Then who is it?" finished Johnson.

It spite of the circumstance, it was comical.

"Her name was Brenda. Don't know her last name; could be she didn't know it, either. She's been down here so many times I'm surprised she didn't have her own office. Street hustler, shoplifter, pickpocket. Hung around the bus station a lot, and at the airport when she could get out there, grabbing anything not tied down if you looked away for a second. I guess Tina wasn't looking."

"So you're saying she lifted Mrs. Pazzo's bag?" asked Johnson.

"It's a possibility, a supposition if you will."

When I'm forced to repeat myself I try to be eloquent.

"Do you suppose that her death had anything to do with Tina Pazzo?"

"No. I'd be looking for a pimp Brenda held out on or a john she ripped off. And if I might be so presumptuous as to give advice to a couple of consummate professionals, it would be real smart to leave Crazy Al out of the recipe."

"Do you think Mrs. Pazzo will report the theft of her handbag?"

"Was there any money in it?"

"None," said Johnson.

"Then I doubt it."

"Do you have any idea where Mrs. Pazzo

may have been when the theft took place, or where she might be now?" asked Lopez.

"No. I haven't seen her in a very long time, remember?"

They gave each other that goofy look again and no one spoke for a good thirty seconds.

"If there's nothing else," I said, "I haven't had dinner."

"Go," said Johnson, "but we may have more questions for you at a later date."

"Anytime," I said, and then turning to Lopez added, "Care to join me for a bite to eat, Lieutenant?"

When she didn't answer, I turned to leave.

"Mr. Diamond," she said.

I stopped and slowly spun around, putting on my most charming smile and hoping she would ignore my hair.

"Would you like this?" she asked, holding up Tina's envelope.

Seventeen

When I walked back up to the front entrance I found Joey Russo in a heated argument with the night desk sergeant. I quickly moved to break it up and ushered Joey out of the building.

"You come to pick me up, get locked up yourself?" I asked Joey.

"The asshole wouldn't tell me where you were. Put them behind a desk five feet in the air and they get all uppity. I remember that clown when he walked a beat and he would give up his wife's bra size for two bucks. Tell me it wasn't Tina."

"It wasn't Tina. Any idea where she was headed?"

"Mexico. She said she'd get in touch with you and let you know where to send her money. Need a ride home?"

"I could use a bite. Haven't had anything I could digest all day."

"There's an all-night diner just up the

street makes a roast beef sandwich that's fairly safe."

"Sound's perfect," I said.

As hungry as I knew I was, and as good as the roast beef was, I picked at it like a finicky cat. As much as Joey Russo disliked getting too personal, my condition must have left him little choice.

"You look terrible, Jake. And I don't mean just your hair. Anything I can do to help?"

"You do enough to help, Joey."

"Jake, remember last year when I called on you for assistance, asked you to pick up a guy at the airport and keep him under wraps for a few days?"

"It was no big deal, Joey."

And he paid me well for it, in cash.

"It was a very big deal; you just didn't know it. I won't burden you with the details, but you actually saved his life. And his life is as important to me as my own. On top of that I may have put you in danger, and I have the Catholic guilt thing pretty bad."

I looked at Joey and saw that he had said all he was going to say about that particular occasion. Not knowing how to respond, I simply remained silent.

"Thing is, Jake, I don't have all that many friends that aren't in it for their own benefit. You, on the other hand, always want to argue when I offer help. Don't tell me I do enough, Jake. When I volunteer to lend you a hand, do me a favor; just say thanks or no thanks."

"Sure."

"Good. Now, at the risk of being redundant. Anything I can do for you? You're sitting there like you don't know whether to shit or wind your wristwatch."

"I'm stuck on trying to find out who killed Jimmy Pigeon and the thing is taking me off on tangents in every direction. I have no idea if I'm getting closer or further away."

"What's worrying you most?"

"I'm not even sure I know. Jimmy Pigeon had a wife. He walked out on her years ago, but I guess he came around to trying to do the right thing. Jimmy was sending money and he left her half the Internet company. Now I don't know if the company is worth a plug nickel; I'm trying to find out. But in the meantime, I wonder if the woman knows anything. And even more than that, if she might be in danger. If Jimmy's death had anything to do with the company, then his murder, and Harding's for that matter, may not be the end of it."

"And you don't know how to find her," said Joey.

"Right."

Joey could read me like a road map.

"Have any leads at all?"

"I'm sure Dick Spencer knows, but Spencer doesn't want to tell me. Even if he did, he's having trouble speaking at all right now, and on top of that, Sally won't let me near him. It's also possible that Ray Boyle knows who and where she is. But getting it out of Ray would take hypnotism."

"I'll see what I can do," he said, and then before I could open my mouth he added, "Thanks or no thanks?"

"Thanks," I said.

"So stop worrying for the rest of the night and finish the sandwich so I can drop you off at your place and get back to my house before Angela calls Missing Persons."

Joey Russo could be very convincing. My appetite came back and I quickly devoured the sandwich and took his offered ride back to my apartment. I wasn't at all tired, having slept the afternoon and early evening away, so I put up a pot of espresso and settled into my living room chair with Dickens. I had to shove the chair back to its place near the pole lamp; the large recliner had moved almost four feet off its spot as a result of the collision with Sergeant Johnson.

I made sure that everything I would need was close at hand. Cigarettes, lighter, ashtray, cup of black coffee, lemon rind, paper-back. I opened the book to the place I had marked and sat down. I reached to remove the lump in the back pocket of my pants and found myself holding Tina's envelope.

I tore it open and removed the short note.

Jake,
  Jimmy may have been working on some-thing for Tony Carlucci. Be careful. I'll let you know where to send the money.
                                            Tina

It was the last thing I wanted to hear. I managed to resist the strong impulse to call Joey Russo. Joey had told me to quit wor-rying for the night and I absolutely did not want to disappoint him.

I placed the note down and picked up the Dickens.

The telephone woke me; the Dickens book dropped from my hand to the floor, I found myself in my reading chair.

The espresso was ice-cold.

"Jake, this is Lincoln French."

"Hello, Lincoln. Anything wrong?"

"I won't be able to meet with you to-morrow. Something came up. Sorry to call so late; I've been trying for hours. I was hoping we could take care of this by phone."

I wasn't all that surprised. I figured I'd better take advantage of the moment and get what I could from him while I had him on the line.

"I was wanting to ask you about Jimmy's business. Sally said that Jimmy came to you to discuss the potential of going public. I was wondering how you advised him."

"I told Jimmy that it didn't look promising. I had gone over the numbers. They weren't getting all that many hits at their Web site. In fact, the traffic was decreasing. I told him that I didn't think he could find an underwriter."

"So did you advise him to sell to Richman International?"

"Jimmy and I had that conversation before the Richman offer. I would have certainly recommended that they sell. From what I understand it was a generous offer, considering the weakness of their company, but he never asked me."

"You say that a million dollars was generous?"

"Extremely generous. I really can't see why anyone would have been interested at all. A large investment in promotion might have helped the business, but there are far better Internet bargains out there. Richman isn't known for purchasing companies that need a lot of work. He's into the quick turn-around."

"So Harding was smart to want to sell."

"It would have been the smart move. Take the money and run. Find a new hobby."

"So why would Jimmy want to hold onto it?"

"Jimmy wasn't a businessman. For Jimmy it literally *was* a hobby. My guess would be that he had a sentimental attachment to the thing. Of course, there may have been other considerations that I was unaware of."

"So, bottom line, what is the company worth today?"

"I think I know what you're driving at, Jake. You're wondering if the company is worth killing for. I thought about it myself when I heard that Jimmy had been killed, and then Harding. Honestly, I would have to say no. I would say that if you're looking at the value of Ex-Con dot com as a motive, you're looking in the wrong place."

Looking in the wrong place. It came dreadfully close to sounding like the story of my life.

"Are you still there, Jake?"

"Yes, Lincoln, I'm here."

"Can I help you with anything else?"

"Maybe. Do you know anything about

Jimmy being married, years ago?"

"Sure. I remember the girl well. We were all in college at Isla Vista together. Hannah Sims. From Colorado. They were crazy about each other. After graduation Hannah wanted to get back home, teach school. Jimmy thought it would be fun, dump Southern California and be a cowboy. Jimmy followed her to Colorado and they were married. The novelty wore off quickly and he was back in LA before long, beating the streets, drumming up PI work. Jimmy loved Los Angeles."

"I hear she remarried, shortly after Jimmy split," I went on. "From what I gather, her second husband passed away not long ago and Jimmy had been back in touch with her, at least indirectly, helping her out. Now it appears that he left her his half of the Internet company."

I felt I was pushing Lincoln's goodwill a little too far.

"I had no idea. Jimmy never mentioned her after he came back to LA. If you're looking for a name or a location, Hannah Sims from Colorado is the best I can do. She kept her maiden name when she married Jimmy; maybe she kept it when she married again. I guess she did it for her father; there were no boys in the family."

My grandfather would have loved her.

"Thank you, Lincoln. I really appreciate your time."

"Thank Sally. She had to talk me into it. Sally cares about what happened to Jimmy, and so do I. I wish you luck."

I carried the cold coffee to the kitchen and glanced at the wall clock. Three minutes to eleven. I wasn't feeling sleepy anymore, but there wasn't much else to do.

I would deal with Tina's note and Lincoln's input in the morning.

I poured a very generous portion of brandy and took it into the bedroom with the Dickens book.

If I fell asleep in the chair one more time I would need a week in traction.

I read, I sipped, and finally I slept.

EIGHTEEN

Monday morning.

The trip to and from Los Angeles had done a number on me. Something like jet lag without the plane. But I woke up finally feeling nearly normal.

I put up a pot of coffee and jumped into the shower while it perked. I found a loaf of cinnamon raisin bread that Tina had left behind and toasted a few slices. I grabbed the *Examiner* from the hall and checked ball scores. I waited until eight, then called Joey.

"I've got the word out on the pipeline that I'm looking for Pigeon's ex. We'll just have to sit back and wait to see what comes back," Joey said.

"You might want to see if the name Hannah Sims from Colorado narrows down the search any. Though I doubt it."

"OK."

"Then again, I may have new priorities."

"What might they be?" Joey asked.

195

"How about coming over to my place? I can run it by you over French roast and raisin toast. That's if you have the time," I quickly added, realizing that I was talking to Joey Russo as if he were working for me.

"That's all I have is time, Jake. I'll pass on the raisin toast; Angela has a potato and green onion frittata going. Give me an hour or so."

"I'll be here."

"Want an omelet sandwich?"

"No thanks Joey, really; you're doing enough."

"I'm going to pretend that I didn't hear that since I asked you to cut it out. You'll love the sandwich, so save some room. See you by nine-thirty."

He hung up before I could thank him again.

I called Darlene and told her that I wouldn't be down to the office until later on.

"Just don't make it later than one," she said.

"Why?"

"That's when Vinnie Strings starts waking up. And I swear he calls here before he even gets around to brushing his teeth."

I spared her the suggestion that Vinnie might seldom, if ever, brush his teeth.

I was thinking of going back to Los Angeles. I still wanted to check out Jimmy's office.

And I wanted to chat with Walter Richman. There was something about his man Alster that felt wrong, even before I had talked with Lincoln French. When Lincoln said he couldn't imagine anyone offering a million for Jimmy's company it sent up another flag. I'd heard it once too often.

Finding Hannah Sims from Colorado seemed less urgent. I saw no harm in letting Joey's pipeline run its course.

What I was still not sure about was why Grace Shipley kept popping into my mind. I kept trying to convince myself that it was intuition, some sense that Grace could tell me something about Jimmy Pigeon's last days.

What I feared was that I was selling myself a bill of goods, that intuition was nonsense, that what I really wanted was to hear from Grace why she had never said good-bye. So that I could end almost three years of guessing.

A knock on the door snapped me out of it, not a moment too soon.

I was expecting Joey Russo, so I had left it unlocked.

"It's open!" I called. "Come on in!"

The gorilla I had met in front of my

cousin's place in LA walked into the kitchen, with Crazy Al Pazzo right behind him.

"Find my wife yet, Diamond?" Al asked.

"Hasn't been four days yet, Mr. Pazzo."

"I took a chance on checking early; thought maybe you got lucky."

Not lately.

"Is that why you sent someone to make toothpicks out of my front door?"

"I noticed the door. Nice paint job; you ought to think of finishing the job in here," he said, looking at the kitchen walls. "I had nothing to do with it."

OK.

"What about sending your boys over to torment my assistant?"

"I'm not in the habit of tormenting women," Crazy Al insisted.

Tina might disagree.

"From what I heard, your guys tried to put a scare into her."

"From what I understand, she handles herself well."

"She's good at that. She has to be to work with me. Don't bother her again."

"Is that a threat?"

"Take it any way you like. I wouldn't insult you by suggesting that you needed clarification. If you're going to rough me up, let's get it over with. Otherwise, why don't you and your pal sit and take a load off. I could toast up some raisin bread; there's some coffee on the stove."

"There's no need for that, Diamond. I'm only concerned about Tina."

"Sorry. Like I told you, I find her you'll be the first to know."

"And I got a little worried when I heard that she was shot and that you went in to identify the body."

Great.

How is it that these underworld types always seem to know everything that's going on everywhere?

I had no idea what to say.

And then Joey Russo walked in with Sonny the Chin.

"How are you doing, Al?" Joey said. "What brings you around these parts?"

Sonny's attention zeroed in on Pazzo's henchman.

"Just visiting a friend, Joey. How about you?"

"If you're here to give Diamond some grief you'll have to wait your turn, Al," Joey said. "The man owes me big on a basketball game and I need to talk with him a little, help him get his mind straight. You have any problem with that?"

"Not at all, Joey," he said.

Pazzo looked like he actually relished the idea.

"OK. I appreciate it, Al. Now if you'll excuse us."

Joey Russo had nerves of steel. I had been shaking in my shoes with every tough expression I had thrown at Crazy Al. Joey was cool as ice. Sonny and Pazzo's primate watched each other like two cats in an alley. Pazzo looked like he wasn't sure what to do. He certainly didn't look as if he wanted to leave. He wasn't done with me and he would have loved to stay and enjoy the mind straightening.

Joey looked at Al, eyeball to eyeball, and didn't move a muscle.

Pazzo backed down.

"I'll be in touch, Diamond," Al said. "Good to see you, Joey." He motioned to his ape and they walked out.

"He didn't look too happy," I said.

"Let me worry about Al's state of well-being," said Joey Russo.

"Joey."

"What is it, Sonny?"

"The sandwich."

"Oh yeah," Joey said.

He handed me the foil-wrapped hero, which he had been gripping like a club throughout the entire exchange with Crazy Al Pazzo.

"Eat," he said, "and tell me about your new priorities."

I took my time unwrapping the aluminum foil. I was about to ask Joey Russo to jump from the frying pan into the fire and I wasn't in a great hurry.

"Tina left me a little farewell message," I said, handing him the envelope.

I'd had it sitting on the table waiting for Joey to arrive.

Fortunately, Al Pazzo had overlooked it or couldn't read.

"This stamp is still good," Joey said as he removed the note.

Russo read it and then held it out for Sonny to see.

"What do you think?" I asked.

Joey and Sonny were busy doing a non-verbal communication thing.

"I have to be honest, Jake; it doesn't exactly make my day," said Joey. "Dealing with Tony Carlucci will make Al Pazzo's visit seem like a walk in the park with Mother Teresa. I'll need a little time to figure the best way to approach him. Is there any more of that coffee?"

Joey dropped the note and envelope onto the table and walked over to the stove. He grabbed two cups from a cabinet above the sink and brought them and the coffeepot over to the table. He poured a cup for Sonny and for himself and refilled mine. He sat and motioned for Sonny to join us.

"Tell me what else is on your mind," Joey said. "You can eat while you talk."

In an hour we had come up with what might be called a plan.

I would return to Los Angeles to check Jimmy's office.

I would try to see Walter Richman. Try to find out if Richman really knew so little about how his highly qualified staff of corporate advisers, as Ted Alster had referred to them, invested his millions.

And I was also curious to know who else Bobo Bigelow may have tipped to Harry Harding's hideaway.

Sonny would keep his ear to the ground for anything that might come back regarding Joey's inquiries into the whereabouts of Hannah Sims of Colorado.

Joey would work out whatever magic it would take to get Tony Carlucci to talk about his business with Jimmy Pigeon.

"That about cover it?" asked Joey.

"Well," I said.

"Spit it out, Jake, while the iron is hot."

"Maybe you can throw Grace Shipley's

name into that pipeline of yours."

"I haven't heard her mentioned in a long time," said Joey. "Does she figure in this somehow?"

"I really don't know. It's like a little buzzing in my head," I answered.

"Done," Joey said.

I would fly to Los Angeles the next morning. Sonny would take me to the San Francisco airport; Joey would arrange for someone to pick me up at LAX and drive me anywhere I needed to go.

I was feeling guardedly optimistic.

The potato-and-egg sandwich was terrific.

NINETEEN

I made it over to my office by one in the afternoon.

"Vinnie call?" I asked Darlene as I walked through the door.

"If he had, you'd have heard about it from the hall," she said.

I filled her in on the latest developments, including my planned trip back to LA.

"You're lucky," she said.

"How's that?"

"If some paying work actually came along, you wouldn't have all this free time to run up and down the coast."

When the phone rang, Darlene looked at it as if it had teeth.

"Diamond Investigation, Jake Diamond speaking."

"Jake."

"Yes, Vinnie."

"What can I do to help?"

I can be too kind at times.

"Ever hear of a guy named Vic Stritch?"

"Sure. Jimmy used to use him occasionally. All Jimmy had to do was call him, wire some cash, and Stritch would do what was asked with no questions. Most of the time the guy doesn't even know who he's working for."

So much for that.

"Any idea where Grace Shipley might be?"

"Not really. I could sniff around."

"Why don't you do that, Vin. It would be a great help."

"I'm on it," he said. "I'll be in touch."

And then he was off the line.

"That was easy," Darlene said.

"Too easy. Any calls?"

"Your mother called."

"What did she want?"

"What do you think she wants? She wants to feed you."

I hadn't seen my mother in almost two weeks. If I didn't get over soon, she would make my life unbearable.

Not that it was such a joy to begin with.

I called Mom and said that I would bring the wine.

I spent most of the afternoon huddled with Darlene going over accounts payable and accounts receivable.

It was a sad state of affairs.

I gave Darlene the five hundred I was holding for Vic Stritch so that she could at least keep the phone alive. If by some miracle Stritch came to tell me who had hired him to trash my door, I could always offer him my 1952 Mickey Mantle baseball card.

I left the office at five. I walked down to the wine shop and picked up a good bottle of Chianti. I hopped into the Toyota and aimed for the Bay Bridge.

To Mom's house.

Mother Mary.

Mom lived with her younger sister, Aunt Rosalie, in a small two-bedroom house in an East Bay suburb, northeast of Oakland.

Rosalie's son was my cousin Bobby, the film actor.

Pleasant Hill is a place that takes its name seriously. Not more than thirty-five minutes from my door on Fillmore Street, the house on Maureen Lane might have been more appropriately reached in a time machine than in a Toyota. Pleasant Hill was as close to downtown San Francisco as Mayberry was to Gotham City.

Mary had moved out west from New York seven years earlier, shortly after my father passed away, to share the house with her widowed sister. Rosalie's husband had been killed when a large portion of ceiling in his Oakland loan office crushed him as he sat behind his desk working a refinance. Rosalie lived off her husband's life insurance and the proceeds from the sale of the mortgage business.

I found Mom in the kitchen, which was like finding George Bailey in Bedford Falls. She was slicing thick pieces of tomato for a salad; a large pot of red sauce was simmering on the stovetop. The first thing my mother did when she moved into Aunt Rosalie's house was have the electric range pulled out, junked, and replaced with a gas stove. Mary claimed she couldn't even boil water on electric. On the burner beside the sauce, water was boiling for the pasta.

"What are you burning, Mom?"

"Don't be cute, Jacob. Make yourself useful and turn the pork chops in the oven before they do burn."

I grabbed a fork and moved to the oven to flip the chops. Mission accomplished, I dipped a hunk of Italian bread into the sauce pot for a quick taste.

"Stop that, Jacob. You'll ruin your appetite."

"Ragu or Prego?" I asked.

"Jacob, I'm going to hit you with this cu-

cumber. Open that nice bottle of wine you brought with you."

"I hope you're not in a bad mood, Ma, because I came over to get cheered up."

"I'm not in a bad mood, Jacob," she said, sounding like she was in a bad mood, "but don't expect me to tickle your toes, either."

"Where's Aunt Rosalie?"

"Out."

"Out?"

"On a date."

"On a date?"

"Is there an echo in here, Jacob?"

"So that's what has you in a funk?" I asked.

"Watch your language, young man. Your Aunt Rosalie is a grown woman. If she wants to go out on a date with someone twice her age it's her prerogative."

"Rosalie is out with a one-hundred-and-twenty-two-year-old man?"

"I don't want to talk about it," she said. "Throw the rigatoni in please, and open the wine already before we die of thirst."

Mom obviously had had a knockdown argument with her sister. Her night was blown and cheery conversation, even if I could scare it up, wasn't going to help.

"Coming right up," I said, hunting for a corkscrew.

"So, I heard that you saw Sally," Mom said, passing the oil and vinegar after we finally sat down to the meal after a half hour of dodging each other in the kitchen.

Darlene had a big mouth.

"Sally's getting married," I said, heading Mom off at the pass.

"And how is your work going?" she asked, looking for an alternative route.

"Fine," I said, sounding like a fifth grader describing his day at school.

We spent the rest of the meal talking about Mom's garden and the plague on her basil. We had cake and coffee in front of the TV, watching the Giants play the Mets.

I thought about my father. The times he had taken me out to Shea Stadium when I was a kid.

Bernie Diamond's enthusiasm for baseball had been equaled only by his enthusiasm for radical politics.

Dad had been a journalist, novelist, and educator. He demanded a lot from himself and expected a lot from others.

But Bernie never imposed expectations on his children. In fact, he rarely questioned us about what we were up to. I had always taken his hands-off attitude as a compliment, an indication that he trusted me and had faith in my choices.

As I grew older I began to suspect that Dad's noninterference might have been due to a lack of interest. That he was too busy with the great social issues, with his own crusades and ambitions, to pay much attention to his kids. And the less interested he seemed, the less I told him about myself.

"Can I ask you something, Mom," I said as I was on my way out the door, "about Dad?"

"Jacob, you know I don't like that kind of question."

"What would Dad think about what I'm doing with myself?"

"Your father was always proud of you, Jacob," she said, with a quick peck on the cheek, "and so am I."

I raced home to ask George Dickel the same question.

After a few drinks I thought I finally understood why Jimmy Pigeon had never told me about his marriage, about staying in contact with Grace, or about Ex-Con.com. Why Lincoln French, Vinnie Strings, Dick Spencer, Tina Bella, and even Sam Chambers from inside the Men's Colony had learned more from Jimmy about Jimmy than I had. And why Jimmy hadn't reached out to me if he was in some kind of trouble.

Jimmy may have simply felt that I wasn't very interested.

It was a sobering thought.

One that didn't have me interested in being sober.

TWENTY

When Sonny picked me up in the morning I was surprised to find Joey Russo with him.

"Tony Carlucci is in Las Vegas until sometime late tonight," Joey said, "so short of visiting his brother John at San Quentin, which I'd rather avoid doing, it'll have to wait."

"All right," I said.

"So I thought I'd come along to LA, keep you focused."

When we reached LAX there were two men waiting at the gate.

"Jake, these are the Fanelli brothers, Jerry and Tom," said Joey. "Boys, this is Mr. Diamond. You work for him now."

The office of Ex-Con.com was above a large drugstore on Wilshire Boulevard. We all went up. The office was fairly large, with at least a dozen computer stations and two executive offices, unoccupied. In fact, the place was entirely deserted except for one pimply kid pecking at a keyboard in the far corner of the main room.

We ambled over looking like the Earp brothers. He stopped typing. He couldn't decide whether to stand or stay seated. If Vinnie Strings had been there, he'd be taking book on which way the kid would go.

Finally he got up and took a few steps to meet us.

The kid was brave. The Fanelli brothers were large.

"Who are you?" he said, trying to sound authoritative.

"A friend of Jimmy Pigeon," I said.

"How do I know that?"

"Because I just told you."

"Why should I believe you?"

Fortunately, Joey Russo decided that we didn't have all day.

"Because Jerry and Tom would like you to," he said.

The kid looked at the Fanelli brothers. Jerry and Tom were smiling and nodding affirmatively like matching bobbing-head dolls. The kid shyly extended his hand.

"Myron Coolidge," he said.

I took his hand and gave it a few pumps.

"Jake Diamond," I said. "I need to look at Jimmy's case files."

"Are you looking for something in particular?" Myron asked.

"I'm not sure. If you could point us in the direction of his file cabinet, maybe something will jump out at me."

"There is no file cabinet."

"C'mon, Myron. Help me out here," I said. "Where did Jimmy keep notes on his cases?"

"It's all in here," said Myron, tapping the nearest computer monitor. "I can bring up a document list, but it's actually confidential."

"Think you could bend the rules a little, Myron?" asked Joey.

Myron took another look at the Fanelli boys.

"OK," he said.

I followed Myron back to his terminal.

"Jerry, go take a look around Jimmy Pigeon's office," said Joey.

"It's the one on the right," Myron volunteered. "His name is on the door."

Hopefully it would help Jerry navigate.

"What am I looking for, Mr. Russo?" Jerry asked.

"Anything that looks like it doesn't belong."

"Where is everyone?" I asked Myron.

"Gone. When Mr. Pigeon was killed,

most of the staff left. After what happened to Mr. Harding, no one came back but me."

"To do what?"

"I'm just trying to handle any requests that come in. Just doing my job."

Who said that you can't find good help anymore?

"Who's paying you now?"

"I'm not sure. The payroll lady is gone."

"What did you get?" I asked, after the kid had searched around for a minute.

"Here's a list of all of Mr. Pigeon's ongoing cases," he said.

I pulled up a chair and sat beside him. I quickly spotted the two names.

"Open the one named Richman," I said.

Myron clicked on the file.

"I'm locked out of this folder. I don't have the password."

"Try the one called Carlucci," I said.

"Locked out," he said.

"Who has the password?"

"As far as I know, only Mr. Pigeon had it. Maybe Mr. Harding. I'm afraid that I can't help you," Myron said, sounding afraid.

Terrific.

"Can't we bust it open, Mr. Russo?" asked Tom.

"No, Tommy," Joey said kindly. "It takes a secret word to get in."

"Like *open sesame*," said Tom.

"Maybe; let's try it," Joey said. He looked at Myron, who was just about to open his mouth but thought better of it and hit the keys instead.

"Nope. Not it," the kid said. "Not a bad guess, though."

"I found this, Mr. Russo," said Jerry, returning with an Express Mail package.

It was addressed to Jimmy Pigeon.

"Why didn't the cops take this as evidence?" Joey said, taking the package.

"It arrived after Mr. Pigeon was killed. The police were already done here," said Myron. "I didn't know what to do with it."

Joey knew. He opened it. He removed the contents. Lots of fifty-dollar bills.

"Jesus, how much is that?" I asked.

"I'm guessing twenty grand," Joey said.

"I don't suppose that there's a name on the return?" I said.

"No name, but there's a return address. Union Street, San Francisco," Joey said, "just down from your office."

"Carlucci's Restaurant?" I said, knowing it was.

"Myron." Joey said the kid's name like it was a prayer.

"Yes."

"You're going to stay here until you figure

a way to get to those files. I don't care how you do it or how long it takes," Joey said, counting out twenty of the bills. "You'll get another thousand when you call to tell me it's done. I'll leave my cell phone number."

He placed the money beside Myron's keyboard.

"What if I can't?" Myron said.

"Myron."

"Yes."

"Myron, look at me when I'm talking to you," Joey said very softly. Myron looked up into Joey's eyes. "I have confidence in you, son."

"Thank you," was all Myron managed to choke out.

"Now get started," Joey said, and then he turned to me. "What now, Jake?"

I really didn't know what now, but before I could say so Joey's cell phone rang.

Joey snatched it out of his pocket, flipped it open, and brought it to his ear.

"Darlene," he said, handing the phone to me.

"Jake, Ray Boyle called looking for you."

"Did you tell him I was down here?"

"No, but you should call him. He said he knows who killed Harding."

"OK, thanks, Darlene. I'll stay in touch."

"Jerry, Tom, go through Pigeon's office,

and Harding's," I heard Joey say. "Look for anything that might be a password. Use your judgment."

"Sometimes people tape stuff on the bottom of their desk drawers, Mr. Russo," said Tom.

"They sure do, Tom. How about each of you takes one office; flip a coin if you can't decide. You can start with the desk drawers if you like. Don't worry about making a mess."

Jerry and Tom started off and I sat at the desk next to the one where Myron was tapping furiously at his computer keyboard.

"How has business been, Myron, I mean apart from the recent executive and clerical vacancies?" I asked.

The kid looked up at me from his computer and then over to Joey Russo.

"It's OK, Myron. Take a break and answer Mr. Diamond's question."

"Not very good. I think that most of the people who bailed out would have been laid off anyway."

"What would you say it's worth?"

"Right now?"

"Let's say a few weeks ago, for argument's sake."

"A few hundred thousand, tops. And then whoever bought it would have to invest a good chunk in marketing to make it pay off."

"Lincoln French was right," I said. "Doesn't sound worth killing for."

"Maybe it wasn't about money," said Joey. "I'll go check out how Tom and Jerry are doing. Myron, get back to work."

TWENTY-ONE

Twenty minutes later Joey and I were back in the car.

Joey drove. Jerry and Tom stayed behind to continue turning the offices upside down and to keep Myron busy trying to hack into the locked computer files.

"Do you think that Richman could be behind this?" I asked.

"With any luck Myron will get into those records and we'll see what Jimmy has to say. Jimmy may have been working for Richman or investigating him. It seems obvious that Ex-Con dot com was fairly worthless; it must have been something Jimmy knew that got him killed."

"Have you ever killed anyone, Joey?" My question surprised us both.

"No, Jake, I never have. It's a lot different now than it was in my grandfather's time; it takes more brains than muscle to survive these days. My businesses are technically legitimate. Of course, the laws of business in this country provide a lot of leeway. I try not to harm innocent people. Territories are pretty well laid out. If no one gets too greedy, everyone does all right."

"There must be times when someone needs a little reminder," I said.

"Sure. So we get together and do some reminding. But there are ways to teach a lesson other than capital punishment, some a lot more effective where it really hurts. Like in the pocketbook."

"So there are rules."

"Yeah, sort of. And if you're asking does Walter Richman play by the same rules, I don't know. He's an outsider; I really don't know much about him. How greedy he is."

"You're a complicated man, Joey."

"I'm a simple guy, Jake. I work hard, I provide for my family, and I try to enjoy myself. That's why I'm here."

"You call this enjoying yourself?" I asked.

"This is fun for me, Jake. You keep thanking me for all I'm doing, but it's you doing me the favor. I get bored. A chance to get away from the backyard grill is a very welcome diversion."

"I doubt that Angela would agree."

"Angela knows that what eases my boredom is good for both of us," Joey said.

221

"Where to? Are you ready to see Richman?"

"Maybe we should see Boyle first. Find out who he thinks killed Harry Harding."

Joey directed the car to Parker Center.

Joey pulled up in front of the LAPD headquarters. He didn't move to get out of the car.

"You're not coming in?"

"Nah, I don't like it in there. Besides, I don't want to get hit with a parking ticket."

"You mean to tell me you don't have a park-anywhere-you-damn-well-please permit?"

"I have one for San Francisco, but not for down here. Angela's brother Giovanni is working on it."

"OK. I won't be long."

"I'll be here."

As I walked to the entrance of the police station, I was thinking about how much I'd come to know Joey Russo these past few days. How lucky I was to have his help, since I would have been useless without it. And how undeserving I felt.

I'd never really gone out of my way for Joey. Part of it was that he never asked and I talked myself into believing that I would be offending Joey if I suggested that he couldn't handle his affairs alone. I was shy to ask Joey if he wanted help, whether he needed it or not.

Joey probably got that kind of treatment all the time.

I was beginning to see things differently.

I have to admit he scared me some at first. Joey had a reputation for being dangerous. I was finding out that it was mostly myth. He wasn't really a violent man at all. There was only one thing that would make Joey a very dangerous man, and that was doing anything that he might consider even remotely threatening to his family.

Joey Russo was a family man first and foremost. Angela nagged him a little too often maybe, but they were crazy about each other. After thirty years of marriage they still reminded me of high school sweethearts.

Walking into Parker Center, I was feeling something that I hadn't felt in a very long time. I felt that I had a real friend.

I would try to be one in return.

When I walked into Boyle's office he set the tone immediately.

"Why am I not surprised to see you back in my little town, Diamond?"

Boyle acted liked he owned LA. As far as I was concerned, he could have it.

"I ran right down from San Francisco the moment I heard that you broke the Harding case, Ray."

"Back off, Jake. I'm not in the mood."

That was a big part of Boyle's problem: he was never in the mood.

"OK, I'll be good. So who killed Harry?"

"Follow me," he said.

I followed him. He took me into a room with a one-way window looking into a larger room. Bobo Bigelow sat at a table behind the glass, sweating it out.

"Bigelow killed Harding?" I asked.

"No. But he seems to think that Al Pazzo did."

"OK, I'll bite."

"Harding was into Pazzo for a lot of cash. A loan he took from Pazzo, at heavy interest. Close to a hundred grand. Harding was hiding from Al, not us."

"If he was afraid of Pazzo, why didn't he come to you?" I asked.

"Harding knew he couldn't drop a dime on Pazzo's loan-sharking and stay alive. Harry told Pazzo that he would get the money and that he wouldn't go to the police."

"Where was the money coming from?" I asked.

"I spoke to Harding's wife this morning. She said her husband was so terrified by Pazzo that he was ready to jump out of a window. Then out of nowhere Harding got an offer for the Internet business and it looked like his problem was solved, but your pal Pigeon was holding up the deal. Richman withdrew the offer, Jimmy got iced, and Harry took off."

"If the offer was pulled before Jimmy was killed," I said, "then Harding had no motive for Jimmy's murder."

"That's how I figure it," said Boyle.

"And Crazy Al wasn't taking Harry's silence and ability to pay on faith."

"And the slime in the next room," Boyle said, looking at Bobo fidgeting, "sold Harding out to Pazzo."

"Are you going to pick Pazzo up?"

"I have no proof. If you would have given me a jingle when Bigelow clued you to the house on Alvarado, I might have been there waiting for Pazzo with open arms."

Boyle wasn't helping to ease my conscience.

"The Pigeon case is still open, Diamond," Boyle said. "If there's anything you're not telling me, now is the time."

"Look, Ray, I don't know any more than you do. I was following a few leads and they went right in the toilet. All I've really been interested in from the start is finding out who killed Jimmy. He meant a lot to me."

"You can put the violin away, Jake; I'm

tone-deaf. You've been running around here all week and all you've managed to accomplish is getting under my feet."

"I didn't want you guys to settle for Harding and close the book. If I hear anything, you'll be the first to know."

"Why is it that everything you say sounds to me like a load of crap?"

I was afraid that if I said another word Ray would explode, so I just shrugged my shoulders. For a second I thought he was going to pull his revolver and plug me.

"I gotta go, Ray. I'm double-parked."

"Get the fuck out of here, Diamond, before I shoot you."

I turned around and moved quickly down the corridor. I was pretty sure he wouldn't put one in my back but found myself weaving nonetheless. I made it to the main lobby and out onto the street just as Joey pulled up in front.

"I had to go around the block a few times," he said as I climbed in.

"Let me see your phone," I said.

I dialed Walter Richman's number.

"Richman International, Ms. Fairbanks speaking."

"Ms. Fairbanks, this is Jake Diamond. Is Mr. Richman in?"

"Let me check."

"What's the story?" asked Joey.

"From what Boyle got out of Evelyn Harding, the timing on the Richman International buyout offer was a little too perfect."

"Mr. Diamond."

"Yes, Ms. Fairbanks."

"I'm very sorry, but Mr. Richman says he doesn't know who you are."

"Ms. Fairbanks. Do your boss a big favor and tell him that it's extremely important that I speak with him."

"Hold on," she said.

"Mr. Diamond?"

"Mr. Richman. Thank you for taking my call."

"I was told that it was imperative. What is this about?"

"I need a little of your time, and it is urgent," I said. "I was hoping that I could drop by your office."

"Mr. Diamond, I'm late for an appointment. I have to leave this minute. I can see you for a short time this afternoon."

"What time?"

"Two?" he asked.

"I'll be there," I said.

"So?" said Joey.

"Richman will see me at two," I said. "Harding needed quick liquid assets to square a debt with Al Pazzo. All of a sudden someone at Richman International takes an interest in a washed-up Internet business and it's like the cavalry arrived. Then the deal fell through and Pazzo fell on Harry."

"So, we're back to Richman, another little buzzing in your head?"

"It's more like a chain saw. What's going on down there? Money is going in and out the door. No one wants to bother Richman with mundane concerns like million-dollar throwaways and internal investigations. Maybe Jimmy stumbled onto something. And where the hell does Tony Carlucci fit in?"

"Look, Jake. You'll talk with Richman in an hour or so, and with any luck we'll see Tony C. tonight. We can sit here shooting in the dark or we can take a break."

Joey had the thankless job of having to continually reel me back in.

"We have time to kill before your meet with Richman," he said. "How about we do something that has absolutely nothing to do with the case?"

"Do you know somewhere I can get a suit and a shirt?"

"Never knew you to be too concerned about what you were wearing, Jake."

"There's something about LA that brings out the fashion awareness in me."

"I know just the place," Joey said, "and we have just the kind of cash on hand to do it up right."

It was one-thirty in the afternoon. A Wednesday. At just about that time the previous Wednesday I had been clearing my folded underwear off a chair in my office for Evelyn Harding.

Joey and I walked out of the Gentleman Caller's Shop. I was wearing a five-hundred-dollar suit, which was actually midpriced in that particular part of town, a shirt that ran ninety-five bucks, and a pair of shoes like the ones O.J. may or may not have owned. Not only was it the most expensive outfit that I had ever worn; it may have outcost all of my other clothing put together.

"How did your brother-in-law afford locating on Rodeo Drive?"

"When Giovanni first opened, it was more a laundry than a clothing store, if you get my drift. I really love what he calls the place; Giovanni is big on Tennessee Williams. He considers *The Glass Menagerie* the greatest play since *Richard the Third*. Why didn't you pick out a few ties while we were in there?"

"I don't know; it's hard to explain. I just don't feel ready for the ties quite yet. Let's go see Richman."

TWENTY-TWO

Twenty minutes later we were pulling into the underground garage at the headquarters of Richman International.

"I'll wait down here, Jake," said Joey. "I'll check in with Myron and call Sonny up in San Francisco."

"Ask Myron to search the name Alster to see if anything comes up."

As I found my way from the garage to the lobby entrance, I reminded myself why I had come. I was there to get information, not to give it up. If Jimmy had stumbled upon something within these walls that cost him his life, I wanted to find it before it got away from me. I had a strong feeling that the answer to Jimmy's murder was somewhere in this building, and I hoped to keep it here and not scare it off.

I wanted to confirm that Richman knew little or nothing about Ex-Con.com and discover if Alster had told Richman anything about my lunch meeting with him at the Beverly Hills Hotel and his allusion to an inside investigation into one of Richman's employees. At the same time, I wanted to avoid alarming Richman to the point where he might call in outside authorities or start asking questions that might cause Jimmy's killer to disappear.

I wanted to learn how someone at Richman International might personally gain from offering much more for Ex-Con.com than it was worth. At the same time, I didn't want to alert Richman to the possibility that someone may have been trying it.

I took the elevator up to Richman's suite of offices. When I walked into the reception area, Ms. Fairbanks looked almost pleased to see me. It was a refreshing change since lately everyone but Joey had been treating me like a contagious disease.

"That's a very handsome suit, Mr. Diamond," she said.

"Thank you. Christmas in July. Can I see Mr. Richman?"

"Go right in," she said, indicating the huge oak double doors behind her. "Can I bring you coffee or a drink?"

"No, thank you," I said, and entered Richman's office.

"Please sit down, Mr. Diamond. Can I offer you a drink?"

"With all due respect, Mr. Richman, I want to get straight to the point. I know your time is valuable, and I'm in a bit of a rush myself. It would be helpful if you would just try to answer my questions with answers and not more questions."

"Go ahead."

"What was your interest in Ex-Con dot com?"

"Ex-Con dot com? I wasn't aware that I had any."

"Mr. Richman, your company recently made an offer of a million for a takeover."

"Mr. Diamond, I must have signed checks for thirty million dollars in the past few months alone, and we have taken in perhaps twice that much," Richman said. "I have people all over the world making deals, buying up companies and selling them, sometimes in the same day. Are you sure I can't interest you in some kind of refreshment?"

I doubted that any kind of refreshment was in my horoscope.

"Positive, Mr. Richman; please go on."

"Aside from my film interests, I don't pay much attention anymore. I trust my people, and when something comes across my desk

I usually just sign it. If I have a few minutes to spare I might even read it."

I was way out of my element. I thought about sneaking a requisition for a case of Mylanta past him.

But it was pretty much the way Alster had run it by me.

"That's very interesting, Mr. Richman, but not particularly helpful."

"You say we made an offer for this company."

"Yes."

"Is an offer still pending?"

"No, it was withdrawn."

"Who did the research for us?"

"Mr. Alster," I said, for lack of any other name.

"Ted Alster is one of my best corporate lawyers, Mr. Diamond. Alster does his homework. I'm sure that Ted could determine if it was a good investment or not."

Everyone I had spoken to claimed that it was a poor investment from the get-go, including Alster. It was sounding as if Ted Alster hadn't gotten around to bothering Mr. Richman with the so-called in-house investigation.

I cautiously dropped in a line.

"Are you aware that Alster had a meeting with me last week?"

233

"No. What was it about?"

I guess that settled it.

What I really needed to know was the name of the other associate, the man who had initiated the offer to begin with. Something was telling me to tiptoe around the issue. It seemed as if Richman wasn't going to be able to help me, that I would have to try to coax it out of Alster somehow. I'd never been game hunting, but from what I knew it was best not to sneeze when you neared the target. I tried sneaking in the back door.

"Mr. Richman, would anyone in your company offer to buy a small business for a lot more than it was obviously worth?" I asked. "For a tax write-off, perhaps, or on intuitive speculation?"

"We don't work on intuitive speculation at Richman International. We work with hard numbers and factual knowledge. As far as tax write-offs are concerned, that's one area where I make decisions exclusively. Are you driving at something, Mr. Diamond?"

"You were going to let me ask the questions. Does the name Jimmy Pigeon or Harry Harding mean anything to you?"

"No, should it?"

"No, I suppose not," I said, more to myself.

The phone on Richman's desk rang.

"Certainly, Susan, you can leave now. I won't be needing you any longer today," Richman said to Ms. Fairbanks after a short pause. "Please switch to the answering service before you go."

"I guess I'll be leaving also," I said.

"If you have information about any of my associates that might put into question his or her integrity I would appreciate knowing about it, Mr. Diamond. I give my people a great deal of freedom with our finances."

"I really don't know anything of the sort, Mr. Richman," I said, throwing it away. "But generally speaking, you might want to pay more attention to what comes across your desk from now on."

I could see I wasn't going to get much further talking with Richman.

"Mr. Diamond, I'm beginning to feel very uncomfortable talking with you. I don't really know who you are or why you are here," Richman said. "Perhaps this is a matter for the police."

Richman was trying to make me sneeze.

I decided it was time to back off.

"I don't see any reason for that, Mr. Richman. I came hoping to pick up some business acumen. I guess I came to the wrong person."

"I don't understand," he said, sounding as if he'd never used those three words together in a sentence before.

"I'd go into more detail if I thought you were at all interested. Maybe I'll tell you more about it when I'm ready to sell the movie rights," I said. "Is Mr. Alster available? There were a few things I neglected to ask him when we met last week."

"I believe Ted is out of the office."

"Will he be back today?"

"I don't know. But he may be checking in by phone."

"If Alster does get in touch I'd appreciate a call from you," I said, giving him Joey's cell number, "and please don't mention our chat to him."

I rose to leave but couldn't resist picking up the statuette from his desk.

"Is this what I think it is?"

"We received it for Best Cinematography in 1974."

"Was that *Godfather II* or *Chinatown*?"

"*The Towering Inferno*."

"Oh," I said, putting it back on the desk and leaving the office.

When I passed back through the reception area Ms. Fairbanks was gone.

I went down to the garage and got into the car beside Joey.

"Has Myron come up with anything?" I asked.

"Don't worry about Myron; he'll call if he gets something."

The cell phone rang.

"Speak of the devil," he said, and handed me the phone.

"What did he mean by that?"

"It's just an expression, Myron. Tell me you found the password."

"No."

"Did you get any hits on Alster?" I asked.

"No luck. Did you think it was the password? Because I could play around with it a little, if it's an abbreviation or a company name."

"It's just the name of a guy I'm interested in, Myron. I thought Jimmy might have referred to him. But play around all you want. We need something, and quick."

I handed the phone back to Joey and he pulled out of the parking garage.

"Where to?" asked Joey.

"Let's find a drugstore; I need a bottle of Mylanta."

Joey found a convenience store. He handed me a fistful of cash and I hopped out. When I came back to the car he got right to it.

"I've got some good news," said Joey.

"I could use some good news," I said.

"Grace Shipley is out at her friend Evelyn's house."

I wasn't sure how good the news really was.

TWENTY-THREE

"Did Sonny find Grace?" I asked, as we drove out to Beverly Hills.

"Actually, it was your friend Vinnie Strings. He called Darlene and Darlene called me while you were shopping for antacid."

"I'll be damned," I said.

"It is curious," said Joey. "I wouldn't think that Vinnie could find a coffee bean in a bowl of rice."

We pulled up in front of the Harding house.

"I'll sit this one out, Jake, if you don't mind," said Joey. "And Jake."

"Yes?"

"Remember why you're here," Joey said. "Don't forget that it's about Jimmy Pigeon."

I wasn't sure that I would be able to remember anything once I saw Grace again.

I envied Joey a bit, sitting in the car instead of timidly approaching the door.

I braced myself and pushed the doorbell.

Grace answered the chime.

We stood looking at each other, as if both of us were wondering who would be the first to speak. Grace was as beautiful as I remembered her to be, but at the same time I didn't recognize her. I felt as if I were seeing her through a pair of eyes that didn't belong to me. She looked somehow out of focus, almost distorted. I couldn't decide how to say hello. All of the things I'd thought to ask her, to say to her for the past three years, they suddenly seemed incidental. It was as if I were meeting a strange woman who might be able to tell me something about Jimmy Pigeon's last days. The strangeness frightened me; I couldn't remember how I had once believed that the woman standing before me could ever have really needed me, or anyone.

I felt a strong urge to turn and walk away.

She finally broke the silence.

"Isn't Joey coming in?"

"No."

"Would you like some coffee?"

"Sure," I said, and followed her into the house and back to the kitchen.

I knew that the only way to keep my mind clear was to get straight to business.

"Tell me about you and Jimmy," I said when we were seated at the kitchen table.

240

"What about me and Jimmy?"

"How often did you see him?"

"After I left San Francisco I came to LA for a while and I needed some help. I looked Jimmy up."

"What kind of help?"

"It's not important," she said. "Anyway, he helped me out. After that we stayed in touch. We both agreed that it would be better for you if my name never came up. I was having lunch with Jimmy a few months ago and he mentioned his idea for the Internet company. I told him that I might know someone willing to invest."

"So you put him together with Harding?"

"Yes. Evelyn and I go as far back as high school. Her husband was looking for something to get into. It looked like a perfect match."

"OK," I said.

"I came down a few weeks ago for Evelyn's daughter's graduation. Evelyn was really upset. Harry was in big trouble over some debt and needed quick cash. Then the offer came from Richman International and it looked as if the day was saved. But Jimmy had other ideas, and before it could be worked out it was too late."

"When was the last time you saw Jimmy?" I asked.

"At the graduation."

"Did he say anything? Talk about any trouble he was in? Anything that might have had to do with his death?"

"Jimmy mentioned that he was seeing Tina Bella again. That could have been risky, considering who she married."

There it was. An explanation for everything. Neat as a pin. So why did I feel as if the pin was poking me in the forehead?

"Did he mention Carlucci?"

I thought I caught something in her eye at the mention of the name. Then again, I was looking pretty hard for anything.

"No," she said.

I was out of questions. At least, questions that I was not too afraid to ask. I finally had an opportunity to maybe settle in my mind what happened in San Francisco when Grace skipped out on me, but I couldn't get my mouth to form the words.

And then it hit me, and it hit me hard. I realized that it really didn't matter to me anymore.

I was beginning to feel as if all the air had been sucked out of the room. I had to get out. I thanked her for the coffee and ran back to the safety of Joey Russo. Joey was standing outside, leaning against the car. I could see the look of alarm on his face when he saw me. He moved to me quickly, as if he thought he might have to catch me before I fell to the ground. I think that if he hadn't grabbed my arm I would have.

"Jesus, Jake. What the hell happened in there?"

I was breathing deeply, trying to fill my lungs. My chest felt as if it was collapsing. I finally calmed myself down enough to speak.

"I don't know, Joey. It feels as if I just woke up from a long sleep and got the shit scared out of me."

Joey asked only one question.

"You want to get out of here, pal?"

"Yes," I said.

We drove around the hills for twenty minutes in silence.

The phone rang again.

Darlene.

"Jake, I just got a call from some guy named Vic Stritch. He said that for five hundred dollars he had a phone number to trade. He said he'd call back."

"Do you still have the five I gave you?"

"Yes. But I have to pay the phone bill."

"When he calls back, buy the phone number. Don't worry about the phone bill, just hope they don't cut the service before he calls."

"OK."

"Darlene, did Vinnie mention how he happened to locate Grace Shipley?"

"He said he got a call from Evelyn Harding."

"Why would Evelyn Harding call Vinnie Strings to talk about Grace? How would she even know how to reach him?"

"You got me, Jake. I'm just relating what Vinnie told me. Trying to figure out anything that has to do with that kid is way beyond me."

"OK, Darlene. Call me the minute you make the deal with Stritch."

"Who is the guy? Is he dangerous?"

"No, Darlene. He's harmless. You could snap him like a twig. Call me.

"Can we go back to the Harding house?" I asked Joey.

"Why not?" he said.

Evelyn answered the door.

"I just walked in, Mr. Diamond. Grace is not here. Don't ask me where she is; I honestly have no idea."

"Actually, I was hoping that you could help me out on a few questions, Mrs. Harding."

"I won't know until you ask."

"What made you call Vinnie Stradivarius with the news that Grace was here?"

"I don't know what or who you are talking

about, Mr. Diamond."

I hadn't thought she would.

"You mentioned to Detective Boyle that your husband was in some trouble over outstanding monetary obligations."

"Very diplomatically put, Mr. Diamond. Yes, I did mention it."

"Do you know who at Richman International originally contacted your husband to express interest in buying the company?"

"No. Only that a man named Ted Alster called to withdraw the offer."

"What happened when Alster pulled the offer?"

"What do you mean?"

"Look, Mrs. Harding. This isn't easy for me, either. I'm feeling a little guilty about not doing more to help your husband. How was Harry planning to settle with Al Pazzo?"

"When the offer was retracted, Harry appealed to Jimmy. He told Jimmy about the mess he was in and pleaded with Jimmy for help. Jimmy was a good guy, Mr. Diamond. As much as he wanted to hold on to Ex-Con dot com, he was willing to help us. Jimmy said that he would speak with Richman personally, ask him to reconsider."

"Did he see Richman?"

"I don't know. What I do know is that

Jimmy came back to us and said that he thought he had found a way to settle the debt with Pazzo *and* keep the company."

"But he didn't say how?"

"No, he didn't specify; he just told us he had an idea. Then he asked Grace to take a ride with him; he didn't say where, which I thought was curious."

Good word for it. I waited for her to continue.

"When Jimmy brought Grace back he told Harry that it was going to work out, that was all that really mattered," she said.

"And?"

"The next night Jimmy was killed, and Harry ran."

"Grace was here less than twenty minutes ago, do you think she'll be back?" I asked.

"I really don't know."

"I'd like to talk with Grace again, Mrs. Harding. If you hear from her maybe you could ask her to give me a call."

I turned to leave.

"Jake."

The use of my first name surprised me.

"Yes, Mrs. Harding."

"As much as I would like to blame someone else for Harry's troubles, he created them himself. I don't really think that you or anyone else could have done anything to save him. Jimmy Pigeon tried, and I just hope that it didn't get Jimmy killed. If there is anything I can do to help you find out what happened to Jimmy, trust me I will."

"Thank you, Evelyn," I said.

I went back to the car.

"Well?" asked Joey.

"Jimmy was working on a plan to square Harry's debt with Pazzo without having to sell the company," I told Joey. "Boyle said that Harding was into Pazzo for a hundred thousand. How would Jimmy have pulled that off?"

"Carlucci?" said Joey.

"It's all I can come up with. The twenty grand that came in the mail had to be a down payment. Whatever Jimmy was doing for Carlucci had to be worth a lot more to Tony if it was going pay off Pazzo to get Harry off the chopping block."

"We'll see Tony when he gets back from Vegas," said Joey.

"I've got this bad feeling that I'm being played like a fiddle. I just can't sort it out," I said. "I couldn't picture Evelyn calling anyone, least of all Vinnie Strings, to casually mention that Grace was back at the Harding house. I'm thinking that it had to be Grace who called Vinnie, that she wanted me to find her."

"Why?"

"I have no idea. And now she's gone again."

"What do you want to do?"

"I don't know. I'm waiting for Myron to find something. I'm waiting to hear what Vic Stritch has to offer."

"And?"

"And I'm really hungry. I suppose we could grab something to eat."

"Now you're talking," said Joey, "and I know just the place."

Joey Russo always did.

After a pound and a half of steak, a baked potato, and three or four beers I was ready for a nap. We were working on coffee and dessert when Joey's cell phone went off.

"Darlene," Joey said, handing me the phone.

"Jake, Stritch just left. I gave him the five hundred; he gave me a phone number. He said it was the number of the guy who hired him to demolish your door."

"Did he say how he got it?"

"He said the guy called him again, wanted Stritch to keep an eye on you for a few days. Vic has caller ID. He decided that he'd rather sell the number to you than take the job and have to deal with Sonny the Chin."

"Let me have the number."

"I already called the number, Jake. It was Richman International," said Darlene, "and you'll never guess who answered the telephone."

"C'mon, Darlene. I don't need any more suspense."

"Ray Boyle."

"What the hell was Ray Boyle doing there answering the phone?"

"I don't know. I didn't ask. I hung up."

"OK, Darlene. Let me know if you hear anything."

"Something else. Sonny called. He's been trying to reach Joey and having trouble getting through," she said.

"The contract on my door came out of Richman's office," I said, handing Joey the phone. "Give Sonny a call; he's been trying to reach you."

"Do you want to go back to Richman's, try to find out who hired Stritch?" asked Joey after he had talked with Sonny.

"Ray Boyle is over there; God knows why. I'd rather stay away until we know what's up."

"Sonny said that he may have a line on Jimmy's ex-wife, that she may be in California, north of San Francisco. I was thinking we should get back up there," said Joey. "Maybe we can get to see Tony Carlucci tonight."

We headed back to Jimmy's office.

TWENTY-FOUR

Tom Fanelli dropped us in front of the airline terminal. We had left Myron back at the Internet company napping on the sofa in Harding's office. Jerry was still going through Jimmy's office. Joey sent Tom back with instructions to wake the kid and baby-sit him for as long as it took.

"Pick up some food for yourself, Jerry, and the kid on your way back," Joey said.

Joey had called ahead to the airlines; the tickets were waiting for us at the gate. We made it onto the plane with no time to spare.

Twenty minutes later we were in the air and Joey had ordered bourbons. We had to settle for Jack Daniel's.

I thought about Grace. How apprehensive I had been about seeing her again after almost three years. How when I did see her it was not what I had expected.

When Grace skipped on me she had left a short note: *"The trouble with you, Jacob, is that you never seem to know what the trouble is.* "If she had meant it as constructive criticism, it didn't do me much good at the time.

I tried finding her for a while with no luck. Not one of our mutual acquaintances was willing or able to give me a lead. Those who had remained loyal to Sally probably figured that I had it coming.

Thing is, all this time I'd been working under the assumption that I was still in love with Grace. Not obsessed, or anything that gothic, but definitely carrying a torch. It was no wonder I was plugging us into the Dickens novel in my dreams.

Then I finally saw Grace at Evelyn's that afternoon and discovered that the feelings were simply not there. I wasn't in love with her. And here's the really funny part. Since I'd seen Sally at the hospital it was Sally who was drifting in and out of my mind the past few days. Maybe *funny* isn't the right word.

"Jake?" said Joey, snapping me out of my reverie. "Want another drink?"

"Why not? Damn, I wish I'd called Darlene before we took off."

"There's a phone right there in front of you," he said, handing me his platinum Master Card.

I swiped the card and dialed Darlene's home number.

"They're asking for a PIN."

"*A-N-G-E-L-A*," Joey said.

"That's your credit card password?"

"It's easy to remember; she's what I really love most."

I hung up the phone.

What did I love most? My personal identification number spelled *Dickel*, if that's any clue. What did Jimmy Pigeon love most? Mystery, poker, football, movies, vodka, Marlboros, Tina Bella?

I picked up the phone again, but I dialed Myron this time.

"Try Los Angeles."

"What?"

"The password; try *L-O-S-A-N-G-E-L-E-S*. Call my assistant, Darlene, if you get anything." I gave him my office number and Darlene's home number and hung up.

"Los Angeles?" said Joey Russo.

"It's worth a shot."

I called Darlene at the office.

"Did you miss your plane?"

"We're on the plane," I said. "Have you heard anything about what happened at Richman's?"

"Nothing," she said. "Sonny just stopped in, said he was on his way to pick you up at the airport. I'm heading home."

"You might hear from a kid named

Myron," I said. "If he does call, take down everything he has to say. I'll call you later at home."

"Thanks for the warning," she said.

We were making our approach to San Francisco International.

Twenty minutes later we were on the ground.

When we came off the plane Sonny was waiting for us and, though he didn't know it, he wasn't alone. They must have followed him from my office. They swooped in on me like hawks on a field mouse.

"Jake Diamond, you're under arrest for the murder of Walter Richman," said Sergeant Johnson, the handcuffs out and ready. "You have the right to remain silent."

"Silent, my ass; what are you, insane?"

"Calm down, Mr. Diamond," said Lieutenant Lopez. "Let's not cause a scene. And you men, move away please."

Joey and Sonny looked at each other and took a step back.

"OK, I'm calm. Can you tell me what the hell you're talking about?"

"Walter Richman was killed in his office. His assistant, Susan Fairbanks, said that you were in with Richman when she left this afternoon."

"Richman was alive when I left his office.

254

I don't even own a gun."

"Richman wasn't shot, Diamond; he was bludgeoned to death. With an Oscar statuette," said Johnson. "Now let me see your hands."

I let him see my right, very close up. He hit the floor like the ton of bricks he was. I'd never slugged anyone like that before, and I thought I'd broken the hand. Then I was running. I could hear Lopez yelling behind me. I wasn't afraid that she would shoot, but I was sure that some airport rent-a-cop or mindless bystander was going to throw a tackle on me. To my amazement I made it outside without incident and jumped into a standing cab.

"Downtown," I said, "on the double."

The cabbie pulled out into the exiting traffic.

"On the double. I like that, on the double," I heard him mumble.

And we were on our way into the city.

I knew that I wouldn't take the rap for killing Richman, even though they were going to find my prints on the murder weapon. I gave Ray Boyle a lot more credit than that. At the same time, I didn't want to be sitting in a jail cell at Vallejo Street while it was all ironed out.

I wasn't sure where to go. I thought about

255

Carlucci's Restaurant, thinking that Joey might look for me there. But I had no way of knowing if Tony Carlucci would be back from Las Vegas, and if he was back I didn't want to deal with him before Joey showed up. Besides, it was too close to my office.

The cops could be watching my apartment, Joey's place, Vinnie's, Darlene's, and maybe my mother's as well.

Traffic was heavy and getting heavier the closer we came to the ballpark. I could see Pac Bell Stadium from the window of the cab, all lit up for a game. The Mets were in town, the third of a three-game series. I was tempted to change my destination and try to scalp a ticket to the ball game. Getting lost in a crowd of fifty thousand Giant fans sounded like a fine idea.

After passing the exit to the stadium the driver pushed the cab to sixty-five miles an hour.

"On the double," he mumbled. "I like that."

When we got into town I asked the driver to stop at a pay phone. I called Darlene.

"Jesus, Jake. Where are you? Your face is plastered all over the TV."

I should have kept up the dues on my SAG card.

"I'm in a phone booth on Van Ness."

"What if your mother calls?"

Only Darlene would think of that.

"Tell her I said, *'Top of the world, Ma.'* She'll know what it means."

"Jake."

"I don't know, Darlene. Just tell her I'm innocent."

"The news says that your prints are all over the murder weapon. An Academy Award, Jake?"

"It's a long story. Did Myron call you?"

"Yes. He said that Los Angeles did the trick. I don't even want to know what that means. He said he'd wait at the office for thirty more minutes; after that you can reach him at home."

She gave me the number.

"And Sally called," Darlene added.

"Sally?" I said.

"She's at her house in the Presidio; she was tired of hanging around the hospital in LA. She saw the news and called to let you know that if you need a place to lay low you can go there."

How do you like that.

"I was planning to come over to your place."

"Not a good idea," she said. "Two police cruisers just pulled up in front."

"OK, I'll get in touch. Stay calm."

"Yeah, sure. Maybe you should turn yourself in, Jake, before some gun-happy cop stumbles across you."

"Can't do it, Darlene. I can't clear myself from a jail cell."

I was beginning to sound like Harry Harding.

"I have to get the door. Be careful, Jake."

"Presidio," I said to the driver when I got back into the cab. I gave him Sally's address.

FRENCH
LESSONS

There's no big mystery about life, Jake.

It's what happens.

— SALLY FRENCH

TWENTY-FIVE

We pulled up in front of the house where Sally and I had spent two shaky years of marriage. I reached for my wallet. I opened it and found three bucks. The meter read $28.75. My panic level was cranked up a few notches and then I remembered that Joey had handed me a fistful of bills when we stopped for the Mylanta. I reached into the jacket pocket of my expensive suit and took out the cash. I was happy to find the bottle there also.

"If someone happened to ask, would you have to tell them where you dropped me off?"

"Not necessarily," the driver said.

I handed him two fifty-dollar bills.

"I dropped you off at Fisherman's Wharf."

I handed him two more.

"I dropped you off at the Greyhound terminal in Oakland."

I got out of the cab, took a quick swig

from the bottle of Mylanta, and walked up to Sally's door.

"Jesus, Jake. You look like shit. Nice suit, though," she said. "Come in."

I followed her into the kitchen.

"Are you hungry?" Sally asked.

"No. I had a big steak not long ago."

"Those things will kill you, Jake."

"If the cops don't kill me first."

"What's this all about?"

"It's a misunderstanding, Sally. It'll work out. I just have too much to do right now to wait it out in custody. I appreciate your help."

"Don't mention it."

"I've been wanting to talk to you about a few things, about what went down three years ago."

"Don't mention it," she repeated. "I'm not up for it at the moment and you have other things to worry about. How can I help?"

"Maybe some coffee, and a phone."

"I'll put some up. Use the phone in the study."

I called Joey Russo.

"Where are you?" Joey asked.

"At Sally's, the Presidio."

"Carlucci just blew in. He'll meet us at his place tomorrow at noon."

"Jesus, why tomorrow?"

"Be thankful he'll see us at all, Jake. I had to appeal to his ethnic solidarity."

"Is it safe?"

"It'll have to be. Sonny tracked down Hannah Sims through the Colorado State Teachers' Association. She's retired, living off a small pension and her husband's life insurance up in Sonoma County if you still want to talk with her."

"I doubt she knows anything," I said.

"Whatever. The police are probably watching my place; I'll try to sneak out past them. Meet me at the restaurant at noon; stay clear of your office."

"See you there. Thanks, Joey."

I went back to Sally in the kitchen.

"So?" she asked, pouring the coffee.

"So I guess you're stuck with me for the night."

"No problem," she said. "There's plenty of room."

"Why are you going out on a limb for me, Sally?"

"Because I sense that you're trying to do the right thing, that you're putting yourself at the back of the line for a change. I saw it at the hospital, the Boy Scout in you coming out."

"Trying to find out who killed Jimmy may

not be as selfless as you think, Sally."

"I can see that also, Jake. It's not like I know nothing about you. You're thinking that finding Jimmy's killer will somehow square you. That doing something for Jimmy now will make up for not doing enough for him while he was alive. You might even be thinking that it's time to even the score with some other people who have given to you without expecting much in return. You're hoping that it's not too late."

"Is it too late?"

"For Jimmy, yes. But following through is a noble gesture and a step in the right direction. Look, Jake, I'm the last person that has a right to be preaching to you. I was a spoiled, selfish brat the whole time we were together. But I'm working on it."

"Dick Spencer is a lucky guy," I said, as corny as I knew it would sound.

"We'll have to wait and see how lucky any of us are. For now, I don't think it would hurt for you to try to get some sleep."

It was good advice.

I took it.

TWENTY-SIX

When I woke the next morning, Sally was gone.

She had left a note saying she had work to do and a set of house keys. There was a small Post-it on the coffee maker, just below the on/off switch, that read *"Push me."*

I drank some coffee and looked through the *Examiner.* I found a not too flattering photograph of myself on page 3. The good news was that the short accompanying piece indicated that I was wanted for questioning and not murder.

Fortunately I had slept late and only had two hours to kill before the meeting at Carlucci's Restaurant. Even at that, I had no idea what to do with myself.

I decided on a shower for starters, wishing that I had something other than a wrinkled five-hundred-dollar suit to wear. I went to grab the cigarettes from my suit jacket and found a pair of chinos, a flannel shirt, and a pullover sweater neatly folded on the sofa beside the jacket. I was fairly certain that they belonged to Dick Spencer, but I couldn't be choosy. I'd have to stick with the shoes from Rodeo Drive, because Dick had feet like a ballerina.

Squeaky clean and donned in attorney casual, I left the house at eleven-thirty. The walk would do me good. I circled around, taking Bay Street past Columbus Avenue to Powell and then down Powell to Washington Square. From there I could get into Carlucci's and avoid the avenue completely. I fought the temptation to glance up toward my office and quickly ducked inside.

The clock above the bar made it five minutes to twelve.

The place was already filling up with a lunch crowd.

There was an old wooden phone booth at the far end of the bar, just at the entrance to the dining room in back.

I remembered admiring it the first time I was here. When Joey, Grace, and I met with John Carlucci, before Frank Slater's testimony put Johnny Boy in San Quentin. I headed straight for the phone, trying to avoid eye contact with anyone at the bar or at the tables along the opposite wall. I made it to the booth, sat down, and closed the door.

I decided that while I was waiting for Joey I would call Darlene.

"Jake, where are you?"

"Down the street at Carlucci's waiting for Joey. What do the police have to say?"

"A Lieutenant Lopez and Sergeant Johnson were here this morning. You gave the big guy quite a shiner. Lopez said that she just wanted to talk, that they weren't planning to book you for murder."

"How about for assaulting a police sergeant? Did they say why I fell off the most wanted list?"

"No."

"Then I guess I'll wait awhile to turn myself in."

"That kid Myron has been calling every hour."

"Damn, I forgot all about him."

"He's back at Jimmy's office; do you need the number?"

I was scratching the number onto the cover of the phone book with one of Sally's keys when I saw Joey Russo walk in.

"Gotta go, Darlene; I'll call you later," I said, and started out of the booth.

Joey motioned for me to stay where I was and went over to talk with the bartender. The bartender picked up the phone behind the bar and a minute later Joey was moving toward me. He tapped on the glass door of the booth and I opened it.

"Follow me."

"Myron got into the files."

"It'll wait; come on."

I tore off the corner of the phone book cover and followed him through the dining area, toward a door at the far end of the room. Everyone sitting there looked as if they recognized me. A very large orangutan, who did recognize me, led us through the door into an office. He closed the door behind him when he left.

"Jake Diamond, meet Tony Carlucci," Joey said.

"Have a seat, fellas," Carlucci said from behind a desk covered with paper money of all denominations. "What can I do for you, Russo?"

"If I'm not mistaken, Tony, you were paying Jimmy Pigeon to find someone for you. We're here to ask if you'd like us to finish the job."

"Jimmy had twenty grand of my cash. What about that?"

"I have most of it right here," Joey said, reaching for an envelope. "I had to spend four grand or so, but you can have the rest. From now on we'll work pro bono."

"As in free of charge?"

"And for the public good."

"So what's the catch?"

"No catch whatsoever, Tony. You just answer a simple question and we get to work."

"OK, let's give it a shot."

"Who were you paying Jimmy to find?"

"You didn't come too prepared, Joey."

"Throw me a little slack."

"I'll give you a hint," Carlucci said, turning his attention to me. "The guy used to be married to a good friend of yours, Diamond. A little number named Grace Shipley; my brother John claims she was quite a dish."

I started to say something, but Joey gave me a look that almost made me swallow my tongue.

"What was the deal with Jimmy? Twenty grand is a little cheap for the rat that put your brother away."

"I was going to square a debt with Al Pazzo."

"We'll be in touch, Tony," Joey said, and rose to leave.

I got up to follow him out. Tony Carlucci stopped me at the door.

"Diamond."

"Yes."

"I'm curious. How much does one of those Oscars weigh?"

Joey pulled me through the door before I could answer.

He hurried us through the restaurant and out the back exit to the alley. Sonny was sitting at the wheel of a car behind the place. Joey opened the back door for me and I got in. He climbed in the front passenger seat and pulled out his phone.

"Frank Slater," I said.

"He testified against Johnny Boy Carlucci and they've been hunting for him since," said Joey. "Call Myron."

Joey was taking control, and I was thankful for it.

Sonny drove, heading out Broadway toward Van Ness.

"Myron, what do you have?" I asked.

"The password worked; I got into the files. You want me to send it as an E-mail attachment or fax it to you?"

"Myron, get the needle out of your arm. Give me the salient points and make it fast."

"OK. The Carlucci file. Basically notes on a case Mr. Pigeon was working. He was employed by Anthony Carlucci to locate a man named Frank Slater."

I was praying that he could tell me something I didn't know.

"Did he locate Slater?"

"That's where the Richman file comes in.

It's looks like Mr. Pigeon suspected that Slater was working at Richman International under an alias."

"Any names mentioned?"

"No."

I'd just paid five hundred to Stritch for the same sketchy information.

"Anything else?" I asked.

"There was an entry made the night Jimmy died. Mr. Pigeon had planned a meeting with an Agent Madison. FBI."

"OK, Myron. You did good. Now get out of there. Have Tom and Jerry take you home. Get some sleep. Don't forget to take your cash."

Richman, Slater, Jimmy, Carlucci. The trick now was to connect the dots.

"Slater is working for Richman," I said. "Evelyn told me that Jimmy was going to speak with Richman, about reinstating the offer for the business, to save Harry's hide. Jimmy came back claiming he could get Harry off the hook without selling. He must have thought he recognized Slater."

"So he calls Carlucci to make a deal, asks for twenty grand up front, and says he'll turn Slater over once Carlucci gets Crazy Al Pazzo off Harry Harding's case."

"Jimmy's notes said he was waiting for a visit from an FBI Agent Madison on the night he died," I said.

"Well, here's where we have to start making assumptions. But that's what detectives do, right?"

"You really like this, don't you?" I said.

"Are you kidding? I'm loving it," Joey said. "We know that Frank Slater was in the Witness Protection Program. Let's assume that Agent Madison was handling Slater for the program."

"OK."

"Slater somehow finds out that Jimmy made him. Slater calls Madison, whose job it is to protect Slater's identity. Agent Madison gets in touch with Jimmy, asks for a meeting. Madison hopes that he can convince Jimmy that there are legal and ethical reasons to keep it quiet. Jimmy agrees to hear Madison out; they'll meet at the Internet office. Slater gets there first, not wanting to take any chances."

"And this was all about Slater trying to protect his identity?"

"It was about staying alive. If Carlucci finds Slater, Frank's a dead man."

"But why didn't Slater just ask Madison for a new name and beat it to Montana or somewhere?"

"Maybe he liked working for Richman too much to give it up."

"So Slater kills Jimmy. What must Agent Madison think about that?"

"I would imagine he would be feeling a bit worried about his job," Joey said.

"How can we find Madison?"

"In my experience with the FBI, they usually find you. I can call around; I know a few Federal Prosecutors."

"Is there anyone you don't know, Joey?" I asked.

"I'm still hoping to bump into Madonna one of these days," he said.

"Can we assume that Slater killed Richman?" I asked.

"I'd bet on it. I just can't figure why."

"So what now?"

"Well, I'll try to find FBI Agent Madison, see if I can persuade him to give up Slater's cover. I'll have to appeal to his survival instinct. As far as what you should do, and I know you'll hate hearing it, I think maybe it's time you gave Ray Boyle a call. You need his help, whether you like it or not. You keep saying that this guy Alster rubbed you the wrong way; run it by Boyle. If Ray decides that Alster is worth questioning, it won't be at a table at the Beverly Hills Hotel."

Joey was right on both counts. I did need to cooperate with Boyle. And I wasn't going to like it.

Sonny pulled up in front of Sally's house.

"Maybe I'll call Ray," I said.

"Good. Think of it this way: you'll be helping him. Maybe he'll invite you back down to LA and you can work together, like a buddy thing," Joey said. "Meanwhile, stay out of sight; you may still be a fugitive. Let me know how it goes with Boyle."

"Will do."

"How's Sally?" Joey asked as I climbed out of the car.

"Good," I said, "very good."

"Jake."

"Yes, Joey?"

"I'm just wondering. If Jimmy found Slater, why wouldn't he have told Grace?"

"Maybe for the same reason he didn't tell me about finding Grace. Maybe he figured she'd be better off not knowing."

"Maybe that's it," Joey said. "Call me."

Sonny pulled away.

I walked up to Sally's door, trying to count the number of times Joey and I had used the word *maybe*.

Maybe if I caught up with Grace again I would have to ask her about the car ride that Evelyn had mentioned.

The ride that Grace took with Jimmy Pigeon the day before he died.

274

TWENTY-SEVEN

I walked into Sally's house resolved to give Ray Boyle a call with an offer of help.

The telephone was ringing.

"Jake."

"Darlene."

"There's someone here at the office wanting to speak with you."

A moment later, Ray Boyle was on the line.

"Jake, way to go. I hear you slugged an SFPD detective sergeant."

"It was unpremeditated, Boyle."

"I think I can get Detective Johnson to forget it happened."

"What are you planning to do, offer to give him your autographed photo of Police Chief Gates?"

"See how you are, Diamond? I reach out to help you and you bite the hand."

"Excuse me if I'm strangely more concerned about being wanted for murder, Ray."

"Look, Johnson was overzealous. The SFPD was never told to arrest you at the airport, just to bring you in for questioning. You're clear on the Richman killing."

"Oh?"

"Why don't you meet me at Washington Square in thirty minutes and I'll fill you in," Boyle said.

"Grab me a sausage-and-pepper hero from Molinari's downstairs; I haven't eaten."

A half hour later I spotted Ray at a bench in the park, working on a meatball sandwich and taking sips from a bottle of Manhattan Special. I sat beside him and picked up the sandwich on the bench at his side.

"There's another of these in the bag at your feet," he said, holding up the soda bottle. "This stuff is terrific. Coffee soda, what a concept."

"I would have pegged you for a Yoo-Hoo kind of guy, Ray," I said. "So, who killed Richman?"

"The name Jack Canty mean anything to you?"

"Not a thing."

Boyle was going to take me around the long way. I was fighting the nagging impulse to ask Ray what the hell he was doing in San Francisco. I remembered that patience is a virtue and I needed some points. I took a healthy bite of the sausage sandwich, to keep myself from talking, and waited for Boyle to continue. If the name Frank Slater came into the conversation, I preferred that Ray bring it up first.

"Canty worked for Richman. He was embezzling money from the company. Richman confronted him and he clobbered the old man with an Academy Award."

"Did Canty confess?" I asked.

"We haven't found him yet," Ray said.

"You think he might have come up this way?" It was a logical guess.

"Yeah."

The answer loosened my tongue a bit.

"So, how did you make Canty for the killer? Fingerprints on the Oscar?"

"No, as a matter of fact the only prints were yours. I talked with a guy named Alster."

"I hope you didn't let him take you to lunch."

"I bought him lunch, a package of those cheddar cheese sandwich crackers from the machine outside the interview room at Parker Center."

"Peanut butter?"

"Uh-huh."

"Are you going to tell me about it?" I said.

"Alster said that he was looking into some of Canty's dealings for the company, particularly the offer for Ex-Con dot com. Canty offered Harding a million for the business. Alster found reason to suspect that Canty was going to present it for Richman to sign off on as a two-million-dollar deal and keep the change. Alster also suspected that Canty had pulled it off successfully a few times before."

"So why didn't Alster call in the troops?"

"Alster claims that he took it to Richman and Richman said he would deal with it himself. That Richman wanted to be certain. Alster figures that Richman challenged Canty, determined that it was true, decided to call the police, and Canty whacked him."

"And Alster figured this all out by himself."

"He's a bright guy."

"Yes, he is. Did he happen to say where he was when Richman was killed?"

"What? You don't think I asked him?"

"I'm sure you asked him, Ray. Did he happen to say?"

"Alster has an alibi."

I wanted to ask Ray how he had confirmed Alster's alibi, but I didn't want to raise the hair on his neck.

"Well, there you go," I said. "I'm glad to

hear that I'm no longer a suspect. I appreciate you taking the time to stop by and tell me."

"I'm up here to try to find Canty. I stopped by to see if you had anything to tell me, in the spirit of cooperation. I know that you saw Richman and I know you met with Alster. I'm guessing that your interest had to do with Pigeon's murder, that you couldn't care less if they all robbed each other blind at Richman International," Ray said. "So, what do you know?"

"What makes you think that Canty came up this way?" I asked.

"That's not an answer, Diamond."

Ray was losing a grip on *his* patience now; switching over to my last name was a dead giveaway. I eased my conscience by telling myself that he'd started it.

"Do you know an FBI agent named Madison?"

"I've heard of him. Witness Protection?"

Bingo.

I decided that it was time to take Joey Russo's advice and bring Boyle in.

"I think Madison may have been handling a guy named Frank Slater. Slater testified against Johnny Boy Carlucci and put him in San Quentin. The Feds gave Slater a new ID and immunity for his cooperation. I think

Slater was working for Richman, that Jimmy Pigeon made Slater, and that Slater killed him. If you can get Madison to name Canty as Slater, you should wrap up both cases."

"How could Jimmy identifying Slater hurt Slater?" Ray asked. "Unless Jimmy was going to sell him out to Carlucci."

Since Boyle had answered his own question, I didn't bother.

"So, what makes you think that Canty is up here?" I asked.

"He called a number in Santa Rosa from his office before he disappeared."

"So why aren't you up there?"

"The number he called was a phone booth, outside of a little place called the D Street Deli. The Santa Rosa police are searching the area. I'm heading up later this afternoon. I'll try to track down this Agent Madison in the meantime."

"Ray, when you answered the telephone at Richman International, was it Canty's office line?"

"As a matter of fact, it was. Darlene told me it was she who called. Why?"

"Oh, just another nail in Canty's coffin."

"Do you want to come up to Santa Rosa with me?" he asked.

The invitation almost swept me off my

feet. Then I realized that Ray just wanted to be able to keep an eye on me at all times.

"I'll let you know. Call me when you're ready to go; I'll be at my office," I said. "And call if you get in touch with Madison. Thanks for the sandwich."

I got up to leave.

"Jake."

"Yes?"

I could see it in his face. He was going to thank me for helping him. He'd called me Jake again. It would be music to my ears.

"Speak to you later," he said.

Boyle was as bad as I was.

When I walked out of Washington Square I found Joey Russo standing at Union and Powell looking out past me. I turned back to watch with him as Boyle exited the park at Stockton.

"Darlene called me. How did it go with Boyle?"

"I told him about Slater. They're looking for a guy named Canty for Richman's murder. I think that Ray can handle it from here."

"I put a call in to the FBI for Madison, left a message for him to call me."

"Boyle is going to try hunting him down also; he may have more luck. Did you come down to make sure that Boyle didn't plug me?"

"Sonny found out a few things about Jimmy's ex-wife," Joey said. "Hannah Sims taught school in Lyons, Colorado, north of Denver. After Jimmy left she married a fellow schoolteacher up there; they had one child, a girl. Her second husband passed away six years ago, and a year later she retired from teaching and moved to California, apparently to be close to her daughter in Los Angeles. She took a little house in Santa Monica, where I'm guessing she bumped into Jimmy after almost thirty years."

"That's quite a pipeline you've got going."

"It was mostly Sonny's work; he's thorough. Anyway, Hannah's daughter married and moved to San Francisco, so Hannah relocated again. North of here. Sonny had a heart-to-heart talk with Dick Spencer. According to Spencer, Jimmy wasn't seeing her at all but had Dick send some money up every few months."

"Well, I guess that takes Hannah Sims of Colorado out of the big picture," I said.

Joey didn't say a word; he didn't need to. One look at his face told me that I was absolutely wrong.

"What is it?" I asked.

"Hannah's second husband," Joey said,

282

"his name was Martin Shipley. Their daughter's name is Grace."

My reaction surprised me in that the news didn't really surprise me at all. The idea that Grace was somehow in the middle of this whole business was sadly beginning to look logical. It seemed as if the only surprise remaining would be finding out how deep she was in it.

"Santa Rosa?" I asked, recalling Boyle's mention of the D Street Deli.

"Seventy-five D Street. Sonny's parked at your office with the motor running."

"Let's go," I said.

Sonny sped up 101 North. Joey sat at his side; I sat in back; no one said much along the way. For thirty minutes I had been playing with Boyle's business card, turning it in my fingers, looking down occasionally at his cellular number printed at the bottom. We passed the Petaluma exit and I finally put the card back into my pocket.

Twenty minutes later Sonny turned onto D Street in Santa Rosa. Number 75 was on the right; across the street was the D Street Deli. I asked Sonny to continue to the next intersection.

I glanced at the pay phone outside of the deli as we drove past. There was a small coffee shop at the corner of Second and D.

"The Santa Rosa police may be watching the deli," I said. "Give me half an hour. I'll meet you back here at the coffee shop."

I climbed out of the car and Sonny pulled away. I walked back to the house.

The woman who opened the door would be sixty years old if she had been in college with Jimmy Pigeon and Lincoln French. Her eyes belied her age. I saw immediately where Grace had inherited her looks.

"Can I help you?" she said.

"My name is Jake Diamond," I said. "Jimmy Pigeon was a good friend of mine."

"Is he no longer a friend, Mr. Diamond?"

"Jimmy is dead, Ms. Sims," I said. It was the best I could do.

"Come in, Mr. Diamond," she said.

I followed her into the kitchen, where she invited me to take a seat. She poured two cups of coffee and joined me at the kitchen table.

"I hadn't seen Jimmy for years," she said. "Was it an accident?"

"Yes," I said. I decided that she could do without the harsher details.

"I know who you are, Mr. Diamond. When I moved up here from Santa Monica, Jimmy gave me your name and told me that if I ever needed help I should call on you."

"Thankfully, you never needed to use it," I said.

"I did pass it on to my daughter, however, when she was having some trouble with her husband. That would have been three years ago. Her name is Grace, Grace Shipley. Did she ever contact you?"

"Not that I can recall, Ms. Sims," I said.

"Please, call me Hannah."

"Did Jimmy know that you had a daughter, Hannah?"

"No. I don't know why, but I never mentioned it. I only saw him a few times while I was in Santa Monica. I ran into him quite accidentally, in a supermarket of all places. I saw him once or twice afterward, once just before I moved up here, to say good-bye. I was always fond of Jimmy; he just wasn't made for domestic life. I'm very sorry to hear about his passing."

"Did your daughter know Jimmy? Know who he was?"

"No. I'd never told her that I was previously married. I saw no reason."

"Have you seen her recently?"

"Mr. Diamond, is there something you're not telling me? Something to do with Grace?"

"I don't want to alarm you, Hannah, but I really don't know. Grace's name came up in a case I'm working on. In the course of the investigation I discovered that she had a mother in Santa Rosa and thought you might know where she was. I just wanted to ask her a few questions. It could be nothing."

"Mr. Diamond, I was married to Jimmy, no matter for how short a time. If there was one thing that Jimmy always insisted on, it was that coincidence is seldom, if ever, the right answer. Are you trying to tell me that your investigation, which possibly involves my daughter in some way, brought you to my door and has nothing to do with Jimmy's death? Because if you are, it would cause me to doubt your sincerity."

I told Hannah Sims the whole story.

"Grace was here yesterday, Mr. Diamond," Hannah said after I had confided in her. "As far I as know, she is back in San Francisco. I could call her now."

"I think it would be better if you didn't, Hannah. It's important that I see her."

"Do you think she's in danger?"

"I'm not sure. If she is, I don't want to scare her off before I get to her. If you can trust me, after my earlier duplicity, I'll do all I can to see to it that Grace is safe."

Hannah Sims wrote down a name and address for an apartment on California and Seventh in the Richmond District.

"Grace never mentioned the name

Canty?" I asked, back at the front door.

"No," Hannah said.

"Thank you, Hannah. I'll call you."

"Jake."

"Yes."

"Promise me you won't let anyone hurt her."

"I promise," I said.

I walked back toward Second Street and saw the car turning onto D Street. Sonny stopped in front of the coffee shop and Joey spotted me. I picked up my pace.

"Let's get out of here before Boyle trips over us," I said, hopping into the car.

Sonny drove. Joey listened.

"So, the night you met Grace, the night she happened into Little Mike's?" Joey asked, not much like a question.

"She knew who I was, or at least that I was a PI. She must have followed me to Little Mike's from my office."

"Why? Why not just tell you that she had come looking for your help? Why the deception?" asked Joey.

"That's just one of the questions I'm anxious to ask her. Considering the way she took off on me after the Feds paid her off, I'm thinking that it might just be her nature."

"Where to, Jake?" asked Sonny, pulling

into the southbound traffic on 101.

"She's at an address on Seventh and California," I said.

"Jesus," said Joey, "that's less than three blocks from my house."

"Small world, isn't it?" I said.

Sonny pushed it up to seventy.

I asked Joey for his phone, pulled out Boyle's card, and punched in the number.

"Where are you, Jake?" Ray asked. "I tried calling you."

"Never mind where I am, Ray; where are you?"

"On my way up to Santa Rosa."

I involuntarily slid down in my seat, as if Boyle might spot me across the median racing in the opposite direction.

"That deli you mentioned sits across from the house of Jimmy Pigeon's ex-wife. She doesn't know anything, there's no need to bother or alarm her, but the call up there worries me. Keep an eye on the house."

"Sure. Anything else?"

"Did you locate Madison?"

"I have a call in; I was told he'll get back to me."

Good luck, I thought.

"OK, Ray. Let me know if you get word on Canty," I said, and rang off.

Sonny made record time. Thirty minutes

later we were coming up to Seventh and California. I got out of the car in front of the house.

"I'll be over at my place," said Joey. "Call if you need me; otherwise why don't you walk over when you're done here and Angela will feed you?"

"OK. Thanks."

I walked up the front steps to the door. The name Hannah had given me was Carol Taylor. I found the doorbell marked TAYLOR and gave it a long push.

TWENTY-EIGHT

"How did you find me?" Grace asked when she opened the front door.

"I saw your mother."

"Jesus, Jake, why did you have to bring her into this?"

"I think that you'll have to take credit for that, Grace. Can I come in?"

I followed her down a corridor and into the first-floor apartment.

"Nice place," I said. "How long have you been here?"

"A few weeks. I'm house-sitting for a friend."

"Funny that you haven't run into Joey Russo strolling Clement Street."

"I'm not here much. What do you want, Jake?"

"I want to know about the ride you took with Jimmy, the day before he died."

"I told you that the last time I saw Jimmy was at the graduation."

"I know what you told me; now I want to know the truth."

"*Truth* is pretty subjective, Jake."

"Save the philosophy, Grace. Tell me about the ride."

"Would you like some coffee?"

"I don't really care," I said.

She put some up anyway.

"Jimmy took me over to Richman International. We sat parked across the street from the building. Eventually a man walked out and Jimmy asked me if I recognized him. It was Frank Slater. It knocked the wind out of me. I told Jimmy that it was Frank. Jimmy asked me not to say a thing about it and to stay away from Slater. Jimmy said that he planned to make a deal with Tony Carlucci that would settle Harry's problem with Al Pazzo."

"Jimmy took you over to ID Slater?"

"Yes. Jimmy said that Frank worked for Richman. Jimmy spotted Slater when he went over to try to change Richman's mind about Ex-Con dot com and thought he knew him. Jimmy took me over to verify that it was Frank."

"So Jimmy was going to sell Slater to Carlucci and he winds up dead the next day. What did you make of that?"

"I really believed that it was Pazzo who hit

Jimmy, for messing with Al's wife."

"After Jimmy died, did you ever think of contacting Carlucci to make a deal? To help Harry out of his jam, maybe take a few bucks for yourself?"

"No. You couldn't pay me enough to get anywhere near Tony Carlucci. The guy is worse than his brother John; he scares me to death."

"Why didn't you tell me all of this when I saw you at Evelyn's?"

"As I said, Jake, I didn't think it had anything to do with Jimmy's death. As far as Frank Slater is concerned, I couldn't care less what he does or who he works for as long as he stays out of my life. The guy is protected by the FBI, for God's sake."

"I doubt they'll want to protect him much anymore, now that he's killed Richman."

"What are you talking about?"

"Walter Richman was killed. The police are hunting for Frank."

"Jesus, Jake. Where are they looking?"

"He called a pay phone at the D Street Deli in Santa Rosa."

Grace's reaction was easily recognizable as one of surprise. It was convincing.

"I don't understand," she said.

"I'm not sure I do, either. Don't worry; Ray Boyle is up there keeping an eye on your mother's house."

"I should go up there," she said.

"No, I'm more worried about you. You're safer right here."

"Safe from what, Jake?"

"I don't know. Maybe Slater spotted you with Jimmy. Maybe he's looking for you. Until this is settled you should stay right here and not move. Joey Russo is three streets away; I'll be over there for a while."

I gave her Joey's number.

"Are you sure that my mother will be all right?" she asked.

"Yes. Don't go out. Call me if you need me. I'll let you know if they find Slater."

"Jake, there's something I've been wanting to tell you. About the night we met, and about leaving the way I did."

"Maybe we'll talk about it another time," I said.

I turned and walked out of the apartment.

Two hours later, Joey, his wife, and I were finishing off one of Angela's four-course meals when the phone rang.

"It's Boyle," Joey said.

"Jake."

"Ray, what's up?"

"I just got a call from LA. They just found a body in the trunk of a rental car in the ga-rage at the Richman Building. Richman's receptionist, Susan Fairbanks, identified the man as Jack Canty. He's been dead since yesterday."

"Was it Frank Slater?"

"I don't know. There's no one to ID the body; I'm still waiting to hear from Agent Madison."

"What did Ted Alster have to say?"

"They haven't been able to locate him. Fairbanks said that Alster was in the office until late morning and then left."

"Ray, why is it that this doesn't come as good news?"

"I feel the same way; I'm headed back down to Los Angeles tonight."

"Is everything all right up in Santa Rosa?"

"Yes. I'll make sure that the house is covered twenty-four-seven until we figure out what's going on."

"Ray."

"Yeah, Jake?"

"Find Alster."

"I'll let you know," he said, and rang off.

Fifteen minutes later Joey's cell phone rang.

"I'll let you speak with Mr. Diamond," I heard Joey say; then he handed the phone to me. "It's Agent Madison."

"How can I help you, Mr. Diamond?"

"Listen, Madison. Carefully. Your boy

Frank Slater has killed three people and may be aiming for four. I don't want to hear any bullshit about Witness Protection or cleaning up your own messes. Just give me the name."

"He's been using the name Alster."

"Do you know where he is?"

"Slater tried to reach me this afternoon. I've been out of town. The call came from San Francisco. He left a message that he was in a jam and would call me back."

I shoved the phone into Joey's hand and ran from the house. I made it over to Seventh and California in three minutes. I felt as if I needed an iron lung. I took the front steps four at a time and leaned on Carol Taylor's doorbell. There was no answer. I rang another doorbell and was buzzed into the building. I ran up to the apartment door and began pounding on it. I was about to try a Vic Stritch on the door when I heard Joey's voice behind me.

"Try the doorknob," he said.

The door was unlocked.

Grace was gone.

I sat in one of the kitchen chairs; Joey took another.

"What else did you get from Madison?" I asked.

"Madison never heard of Jimmy Pigeon.

Madison never made an appointment for a meeting with Jimmy on the night Jimmy was killed," Joey said. "Slater must have called Jimmy claiming to be Madison and set up the meet."

"I can't believe that Jimmy let Slater walk right in and kill him," I said.

"There's not much you can do right now," Joey said. "Want a ride home?"

"Sure."

We walked back to Joey's house and climbed into his car. When we turned onto Fillmore Street I saw the black Cadillac sitting in front of my apartment building.

"That's Al Pazzo and his gorilla," I said. "My four days to find Tina Pazzo expired a few days ago."

"You can stay at my place," said Joey.

"Take me over to Sally's," I said.

"Nice outfit," Sally said when she answered the door.

"Thanks for leaving it out for me," I said.

"Come on in," she said. "Sit. Get those shoes off. Care for coffee?"

I dropped onto the living room sofa.

"I could really use a drink."

I was exhausted. Sally came up with a glass with ice and an unopened fifth of George Dickel.

I knew that she didn't normally keep one around.

"So," she said, taking the opposite end of the couch, "how was your day?"

I told her all about it.

"Do you think that Grace Shipley may be in danger?" Sally asked.

"I don't know what to think; I don't know if I can believe a word Grace told me. She's lied from the first day I ever saw her."

"Jake, I don't have to tell you the story of the boy who cried wolf, do I?"

"What?"

"If there's even the slightest chance that Grace is in danger, you have to allow the benefit of the doubt. There's less to lose if you're wrong. I thought I asked you to take those shoes off."

I slipped off the shoes and leaned back into the sofa.

I opened my eyes to find Sally shaking my shoulder.

"It's Joey on the phone," she said.

"What time is it?"

"Around nine-thirty," she said.

I had slept for more than two hours.

"Joey?"

"Jake, meet me over at Carlucci's Restaurant, now."

"What's up?"

"Just get over there," Joey said, and he hung up.

"I'll give you a ride over," Sally said.

I pulled the shoes back on.

TWENTY-NINE

When I walked into Carlucci's, the bartender signaled me to go to the back office. I found Tony Carlucci at his desk. Joey hadn't arrived.

"Joey Russo asked me to meet him here," I said.

"I got a funny phone message when I was out, came in about an hour ago, I thought that maybe you could help me figure it out," said Tony.

What would make anyone think that I could figure anything out?

"It was a message from Grace Shipley," Carlucci said.

"What was the message?" I asked.

"The message was that she had thought about my proposition and was ready to tell me where I could find Frank Slater."

"What proposition?"

"That's the funny part; I never made any proposition. I don't know what the dame was talking about."

"That was it?"

"The message said she would meet me at the Shrine at ten tonight, to make the deal. I'm not about to walk into some kind of trap; that place is real deserted at this time of night. So tell me what's up, Diamond."

The clock above Carlucci's desk read 9:48.

"What Shrine?"

"Saint Francis of Assisi, up the street on Vallejo."

"Tell Russo I'm headed there!" I yelled, and ran out of the office and out onto Union Street.

I ran up to Grant and then down toward Vallejo.

When I turned onto Vallejo I could see the Shrine of St. Francis Assisi just ahead. The huge church and its surrounding grounds were dark.

As I came in sight of the entrance I could see a woman approaching the large front doors. I began running and was about to call out Grace's name when I was tackled from behind and pinned to the ground by what felt like a knee in the small of my back. A large hand covered my mouth and I could feel a gun barrel pressed against my ear. I was afraid to move and afraid not to. Before I could decide, my assailant spoke.

300

"Don't try to get up, Diamond. I'm going to remove my hand; don't make a sound. Just turn your head up and look at me."

His hand came away from my mouth and I could feel the gun move away also. He kept the knee in my back, but I was able to lift my head enough to see his face.

It was Sergeant Johnson. He did have quite a shiner.

"Johnson, what the hell?"

"I said shut up," he whispered. "Get up slowly and move away with me."

He took his weight off and I pushed myself up to my feet. A quick glance at the entrance of the church told me that Grace was no longer in sight. I took a step in that direction and Johnson grabbed my arm and dragged me back behind a tree.

"He's going to kill her," I pleaded.

"No chance. Lopez is too good and we've got men all around the place."

"Lopez?"

"Slater was expecting a woman; the lieutenant insisted she go in. I couldn't talk her down; she pulled rank on me."

"What about Grace Shipley?"

"She's safe with Officer Lombardi in a patrol car down Vallejo; we were lucky and stopped her before she reached here."

"How did you get wind of this?"

"An anonymous phone call tipped us Slater might be here."

"Can I go to see Grace?"

"I don't care where you go as long as it's away."

I turned from him and walked down Vallejo Street.

I spotted the patrol car when I crossed Columbus Avenue. I was within sixty feet and headed directly for the car when the door opened and an officer stepped out. I raised my hands over my head and worked at looking as unthreatening as possible.

"I'm Jake Diamond!" I called. "Sergeant Johnson said it would be all right to talk with Ms. Shipley!"

The officer leaned into the car and then stood up and waved me on.

"Officer Lombardi," she said when I reached her. "Sit in the vehicle. I'll wait out here."

I got into the backseat beside Grace.

"My God, Jacob. They said it was Frank Slater planning to kill me."

"What are you doing here, Grace?"

"I came to meet Tony Carlucci. He called me to offer a lot of cash for Slater's identity. I'm sorry, Jake; the money was too tempting."

"How would Carlucci know to call you

about Slater? How would Tony even know how to reach you?"

"I don't know. I really didn't think of it."

Don't know. Didn't think of it. It didn't sound at all like the Grace Shipley I knew.

"Carlucci never called you; Slater must have. But the question remains. How would he know where to call you?"

"Why are you interrogating me?"

"I'm only trying to understand."

"I said I don't know."

I decided to back off.

"I'm sorry, Grace. You put a scare into me is all."

If Grace had anything more to say she didn't get the chance. A plain black Plymouth pulled up; Johnson and Lopez climbed out. I opened the door of the police cruiser and followed suit.

"If Slater was there, he got away," said Lopez.

"If?"

"We had a pretty tight net around that place," said Johnson.

They always had me wondering if they practiced taking turns speaking.

"Officer Lombardi."

"Yes, Lieutenant."

"Please drive Ms. Shipley home, and stay outside the house until you hear otherwise."

"Yes, Lieutenant."

Lombardi got into her car and then started the engine. I almost called out for her to stop.

The patrol car pulled away from the curb and down Vallejo Street.

I must have looked like a kid lost in a shopping mall.

"Any idea where to start looking for Slater?" I asked.

"Don't worry your pretty little head, Diamond; we'll get him."

Lopez was a tough cookie.

"It took guts doing what you did back there, going in alone."

"I don't know. I had a hunch it was safe."

"But you don't want to tell me about it."

"Right."

Joey Russo walked up behind me.

I really had nothing else to say to Lopez or Johnson. I spotted Joey's car up the street and walked toward it, Joey following.

"What's up, Hamlet?" Joey asked.

"What do you mean?" I said.

"You look like you just caught a whiff of something rotten in Denmark."

"Do you have your cell phone?"

"Never leave home without it," Joey said, handing it over.

I pulled out Boyle's card and called him.

"Ray, where are you?"

"Back in San Francisco. I was waiting for a flight to LA. I just heard about what happened at the Shrine; I'm on my way to meet Lieutenant Lopez there."

"Ray, you know now that Slater was Alster and not Canty. Right?"

"Yes. I had the maniac down at Parker and let him go."

"Don't beat yourself up, Ray. Like you said, he's a bright guy. You told me that he gave you an alibi for where he was when Richman was killed. What was it?"

"Jesus, I didn't think of that. He said he was up here in San Francisco visiting a friend. I called the woman and she verified his story."

"She have a name?"

"Let me see; I've got it here somewhere. Here it is, Carol Taylor."

"Do you have an address?" I was already leaning.

"Seventh and California."

"Ray, meet me over there right away," I said, and rang off.

Joey and I climbed into his car.

When we reached the house there was no patrol car sitting out front and no one at the apartment.

Ray Boyle pulled up in front a minute later.

"Do me a favor, Joey," I said. "Call Lieutenant Lopez and see if you can find out where Lombardi took Grace."

"No one here, Ray," I said, walking over to meet him.

"Who's this Carol Taylor?" Ray said. "Any idea?"

"None."

I knew when I said it that I had made up my mind.

"I'll call for a stakeout," Ray said.

"I'm wasted, Ray. I'm going to try to get some sleep. Let me know if you hear anything about Slater."

I climbed back into Joey's car.

"Did you speak to Lopez?"

"Lopez wouldn't talk," said Joey, "but Janis did."

"Janis?"

"Janis Lombardi," said Joey. "I thought I recognized the kid. Her father, Vito, wears a badge, too; he was an old friend of mine from the neighborhood."

"So?"

"So, after they leave Vallejo, Grace changes her mind and asks to be dropped at a hotel at the airport. Lombardi calls it in and Lopez tells her to do it; they can't keep Grace from going wherever she wants to go."

"Grace is planning a trip."

"So it would appear, but not before morning. I sent Sonny over to the hotel to see that she doesn't move before then."

"Where is she off to, would you think?"

I was beginning to ask Joey questions as if I expected him to know all the answers.

"She charged a ticket to Grand Cayman through the hotel."

And it always seemed to work.

"How did you find that out?"

"Sonny managed to coax it out of the hotel desk clerk," Joey said. "Where to?"

"Frederick Street between Masonic and the park."

Joey turned the corner of Masonic Avenue onto Frederick; Buena Vista Park was a block ahead at the end of the street. He pulled to the curb in front of the house.

"How did you ever manage a find like Sonny the Chin?" I asked.

"My daughter found him; he's my son-in-law."

"I had no idea that you had a married daughter, Joey."

"And a granddaughter, a son in medical school, and another son working for the DA's office in San Diego. There's a lot about me that you're not aware of, Jake. If I didn't know better, I'd think that you weren't interested."

I had nothing to say.

"What's your plan?" Joey asked, letting me off the hook.

"I'm going to catch up with Grace and find Slater."

"And then?"

"I'm not sure yet."

"My father had a favorite saying. It sounds better in Italian, but I'll give you the translation: There's only one way to be, your way and the right way."

"That sounds like two ways to me, Joey."

"That's the trick, pal. Make it one. You know where to find me."

I climbed out of the car and Joey held an envelope out the window.

"Take this," he said.

"What is it?"

"Your expense account; it's almost five grand that I held back from Carlucci."

"Joey."

"Yeah, Jake?"

"What's her name?" I said. "Your granddaughter, what's her name?"

"Carmella."

"Thanks, Joey," I said, and watched him drive away.

I walked up to the door of the house and rang the doorbell.

A minute later Darlene opened the door.

"Jesus, Jake, you've got my hair turning gray."

"Can I come in?"

"Yes, come in, damn it. You have some explaining to do. I'll put up some coffee."

Thirty minutes later I had Darlene up to speed and had told her what I was hoping she would do.

"Where is that, anyway? Near Hawaii, I hope."

"South of Cuba. Northwest of Jamaica. Seventy-six square miles. Five hundred sixty-seven banks."

"Wow, that must be at least a four-hour trip."

"Six hours, with a stopover in New York. Look, Darlene, you know you don't have to do this."

"I don't know anything of the sort. Of course I have to do it," she said.

"OK. We'd better get some sleep; we're looking at an early start in the morning. Don't forget to pack your swimsuit."

"Ever been told you're a laugh a minute, Jake?"

"I hear it every sixty seconds. Get some rest."

I opened up Darlene's sofa bed and was overcome with sadness. It could only remind me of what it was: the bed I slept in the night I met Grace.

It had become impossible to make myself believe that Grace was innocent.

Darlene shook me awake at seven.

"Go take a shower and let's get this show on the road."

I made it a quick one and started dressing.

"Here," Darlene said, handing me a new shirt. "I picked this up for your birthday, I know it's not for two weeks, but it really can't wait. Nice outfit, by the way. What do you call it, attorney casual?"

Darlene loved torturing me and mothering me.

"I should call my mother," I said.

"I already did. I told her you were fine. You can call her yourself if you'd like to be stuck here on the phone for the next hour."

"I guess not."

"Well then, let's get going."

When we reached the hotel, Sonny met us at the entrance.

"She's still up there, Room Four-Eighteen; her flight leaves in two hours. Want me to stick around?"

"No. Thanks for your help."

"Anytime," he said, and was gone.

Darlene and I walked into the hotel lobby.

"That looks like a comfortable chair over there."

"I don't need you to tell me where to sit, Jake. I'll be fine. I brought my copy of *Football Digest*."

"Well, here I go."

I took the elevator to the fourth floor and walked down to the end of the hall. I stood in front of the door, took a deep breath, and knocked lightly.

When she opened the door she hardly looked surprised.

"I finally seem to know what the trouble is, Grace."

She stepped aside and I walked into the room.

THIRTY

"A few weeks ago I was on a flight to Los Angeles; I was on my way for Misty Harding's graduation. I'd been down and out, which was not unusual, staying with my mother up in Santa Rosa for a while."

Grace paused for a moment. I didn't interrupt.

"I was sitting in the window seat on the plane and a man took the aisle seat next to me. I turned to look at him and I almost screamed. He looked different; something changed in his chin and cheeks. His eyes were blue now, his hair longer and darker. But I knew who he was immediately, and of course he knew me. And the first words he said, not *hello, miss* or *hello, Grace*, not *first time visiting Los Angeles?* or *small world, isn't it?* The first words out of his mouth are, 'How would you like ten million dollars?' "

Tough question.

"And you said?"

"And I said, 'What do I have to do, Frank?' And the deal was struck, before the plane ever left the ground. I keep quiet about who he was and he makes me a multimillionaire. Simple as that."

"What made you think you could trust him?"

"Oh, I never thought I could trust him. But he had the trust factor all worked out the moment I took the hook. We would open a joint offshore bank account that neither of us could access without the other, so we would need for each other to stay healthy. For two hours he talked about Richman International. The work he did for Richman, the practice runs, skimming small amounts on business deals, and the big score that would culminate at the beginning of the month. And it wouldn't hurt a soul, barely put a dent in Richman's deep pocketbook."

"It was criminal, Grace. And it did hurt some souls."

"Let me finish, while I still have the stomach for it. Save your admonishments until the end, though I'm sure it won't be anything I haven't already leveled at myself."

"Go on."

"The plan was fairly simple and it hinged

on the fact that Richman paid little or no attention to what his people were doing with his money, since what they mostly did was increase it. Frank set up a dummy company, in both our names, with an account in a bank on Grand Cayman. He would purchase the company for Richman International. By the time Richman found out that he had paid twenty million dollars for nothing, Frank and I would have the money in our hands. The purchase and transfer were set for Wednesday morning. There was a second-quarter audit scheduled the beginning of the week. Once that was completed, Frank could make the move. It could have gone unnoticed for weeks, if not months. But then you showed up at Richman's."

"And Richman questioned Slater."

"Frank needed forty-eight hours for the deposit to clear and time to get out of the country. Frank was afraid that Richman might dig around and have time to stop the transaction. So Frank killed Richman. There was no one else at the office. Then Jack Canty popped in and Frank had to kill him also, and Frank tried shifting the suspicion to Canty."

"Why the call to the deli in Santa Rosa from Canty's phone line?"

"Santa Rosa, the whole charade at the Shrine, was to take attention off Frank and away from LA until he could get out of the country. He needed to go into his office one more time, yesterday morning, to make sure that everything had cleared with the transfer of the twenty million to the bank in the Caymans."

"I need to know about Jimmy."

"It's unbelievable."

"I'm sure it is."

"I was trying to do a favor for Evelyn. I knew that Harry was in big trouble with Al Pazzo, so I asked Frank if he could do something to help. Frank said that he could buy Ex-Con dot com for Richman International and that Jimmy and Harry would do very well. And it backfired. Jimmy was holding up the sale; Frank was afraid that it would bring attention to the bigger scam and pulled the offer."

"Then Jimmy went to see Richman and spotted Frank," I said. "Jimmy decided to go a different route, make a deal with Carlucci, and Jimmy brought you down to be sure it was Frank. Why didn't you just tell Jimmy that he was wrong?"

"I had a strong feeling that Jimmy didn't need my verification. That he was testing me, to see what I would say."

"So you told Frank that Jimmy was on to him."

"I had to. And Frank told me not to worry, that Jimmy was no problem, that he would see Jimmy and offer him more than Jimmy could get from Carlucci if he would give Frank time to get away."

"What possible reason could you have had to believe Frank Slater, Grace?"

"I had ten million reasons."

"And Frank killed Jimmy."

"Frank said that he had no choice and that I was implicated, so I should forget it. He told me to go back to Santa Rosa and wait it out."

"Why me, Grace? Why did you send Evelyn to me?"

"Wake up, Jake. Who else? I sent Evelyn to you for the same reason I let Vinnie Strings know when you could find me at Evelyn's. For the same reason we led you to my mother so you could find me at Carol Taylor's place. You were easy to control, Jake. While you were chasing all over Northern California, Frank was in LA wrapping everything up and jumping a plane to Cayman."

"Who did you think was going to control Frank? He killed three people, Grace."

"I was obviously not thinking about anything but the money. You have to believe that I had no idea that Jimmy would be hurt."

"It doesn't matter what I believe. You'll have to convince yourself."

"So what now?" she asked.

"You tell me."

"I'm supposed to meet Frank at the airport in Grand Cayman. We go to the bank and withdraw the money, split it up, end of story."

"You have two choices, Grace. You help me get Frank or you don't. Either way, you are out ten million dollars, but if you help me it may keep you out of prison."

"I don't care anymore. I don't care about the money, and I'm already in hell. I can't see how prison could be any worse."

I picked up the room telephone and dialed the front desk.

"There's a Ms. Roman in the lobby reading a sports magazine; could you please send her up to Room Four-eighteen."

I lit a Camel and sat on the bed to wait for Darlene.

We went through the plan once and then once again. Darlene was losing patience fast; Grace sat two feet from her but was a million miles away.

There was a knock on the door.

"Sonny," I said, "I didn't know it would be you."

"It was either me or Joey, and my mother-in-law won the debate."

He came into the room and stood against the wall.

"Again, Darlene," I said.

"We get off the plane, I find Slater, and I tell him the score."

"Come on, Darlene. I want you to go through the whole thing one more time. Practice makes perfect and I want Sonny to hear this."

"You're making me mad, Jake. I might just run off with Frank."

"Darlene."

"I meet Slater at the airport in Grand Cayman. 'Mr. Slater,' I say, 'I'm here on behalf of Grace Shipley. And Jake Diamond. Mr. Diamond would love to see you swinging from a tree, but he would love five million dollars just a tiny bit more. I have Grace's part of the information needed to access the cash, and you can't get at it without me.' " Darlene paused a beat. " 'Keep quiet and let me finish, Frank.' "

Sonny was trying to stifle a laugh.

"Go on," I said.

" 'I meet you at the bank when it opens

tomorrow morning' I say. 'We'll get the dough and you can kiss me good-bye. Meanwhile, if Mr. Diamond doesn't hear from me every hour on the hour you'll never get anywhere near the bank.' " Darlene let out a long sigh. "Then I turn and walk away."

I turned to Sonny the Chin.

"And you follow Slater," I said to him. "Go on, Darlene; you're doing great."

"Aw shucks, Boss, thanks. I meet Slater at the bank; we get the money and make the split; I catch my flight to Buenos Aires."

This time I had to laugh.

"OK. I go back to my hotel room and give you a yell," said Darlene.

"And I follow Slater," said Sonny.

"I want Darlene to be safe at all times, Sonny."

"Don't worry, Jake."

"Can we go now or do you want us to miss the flight?" said Darlene.

"OK, get out of here. Be careful."

Sonny and Darlene left for the airport.

I would have to stay in the hotel room for the next twenty-four hours worrying about them and keeping company with a zombie.

THIRTY-ONE

I called down to the front desk and ordered a pot of coffee and a carton of Camel cigarettes.

Darlene called from her hotel in Grand Cayman at eight in the evening. I had spent the last ten hours watching television, reading Dickens, drinking bad coffee, and smoking up a storm. I managed to get Grace to eat something at lunchtime, but her dinner sat getting cold on the bedside table. She mostly stared into space, silently, once in a while lying down, though I don't think she ever slept. It was torture.

"Slater will meet me at the bank at nine a.m.," said Darlene. "Sonny tailed him from the airport; he said he'll call you later."

"What's it like down there?"

"Just groovy, Jake. Especially when you're a gal who just loves to drink watered-down rum and artificially sweetened pineapple juice out of a coconut shell. I'm heading down to the poolside bar to grab a few right now. Take a count of how many college boys tell me what a bitchin' babe I am."

"Darlene, I told you that you didn't have to do this."

"I know what you told me, Jake. Chill out; I'm just yanking your chain. It's really quite beautiful down here. In fact, I was hoping that when this was over I could hang out. Maybe get my boyfriend down here for a few days."

"Sure, Darlene, live it up. Call me before you leave for the bank."

Just before ten, Sonny called telling me he had Slater covered and would call again in a few hours.

Just before eleven there was a knock on the door. It was Joey Russo.

"I rented the room next door, Jake. Thought you might try to get some sleep," he said, looking over at Grace lying quietly on the bed. "I'll sit with her for a while."

"I'm expecting a call from Sonny."

"I'll let you know if there's any problem."

I went into the next room and dropped onto the mattress. I put in for a wake-up call at six. I didn't really think I could sleep, but I was wrong.

The call at six came in no time. I splashed some water on my face and went back to Grace's room. To my amazement, I found

Grace and Joey talking with each other. She looked a lot better than when I had left.

"Good morning, Jake. I was just telling Grace about my grandkid. How she loves hiding my car keys and shakes a finger at me when I try to light a cigar in the house. How about I order some breakfast?"

I looked at Joey and shook my head in awe.

I wanted to be like Joey Russo when I grew up.

"Sounds great, Joey," I said.

Joey's presence had done wonders. Grace was doing an impressive job on the food. Joey had brought some magazines over with him, and Grace was thumbing through them. Joey and I watched the *Today Show* and waited for word from Darlene.

Darlene called at eight-forty.

"Sonny just called me; Slater left for the bank. I'm on my way now."

"Call me as soon as you get back."

"Will do."

All we could do was wait some more.

I nearly jumped out of my chair when the phone rang at ten-thirty.

"Done," said Darlene.

"Where are you?"

"Back at my hotel."

"And Slater?"

"I don't know, but I'm sure Sonny's on him like white on rice."

I knew better, but I asked anyway.

"And the money?"

"Where do you think the money is, Jake?"

"Where I told you to put it."

"I walked it right into the next bank I passed after Slater left. Which was about two feet away from the one we had just come out of. There was a nicer-looking one right across the street, but I didn't want to risk being run down by a bus while I was carrying ten million."

"Let me have the name of the bank and the account number."

"Well, OK, I guess so," she said. I could see her smiling. She gave me the information.

"I can't thank you enough, Darlene. You deserve a little vacation. Is your boyfriend coming down to join you in Paradise?"

"He can't make it, the bum. Preseason training camp. And I don't know how much fun I'd have staying here alone."

"I could send Vinnie Strings down."

"Go fly a kite, Diamond. I'll suffer it another day and fly out first thing in the morning."

"Thank you, Darlene."

"You want to thank me, get a new coffee

machine for the office."

I placed the receiver down and the phone rang again instantly.

"Jake, Sonny. Slater is leaving for the airport. I have no idea where he's headed, but I'll follow all the way. You might not hear from me for a while, so sit tight. And don't worry; I know what to do."

"Thanks, Sonny."

I hung up the phone and turned to Joey.

"So, that's it," he said.

"Until we hear from Sonny."

"And what about her?" Joey asked quietly, nodding toward Grace.

"I guess I'll try to talk to her."

"OK. I'll leave you to it."

He rose from his chair and moved to the door.

"Remember what my old man used to say, Jake, your way and the right way."

He smiled at me and left the room.

I looked over at Grace Shipley.

I was on my own.

It was time to find out what I could handle on my own.

High time.

It had been about greed, one of the seven deadly sins, in this case very deadly. There are those who would call it human nature, the need to accumulate more money or more power by nearly any means. Not to be condoned necessarily, but often hard to argue against and often difficult to resist.

Some have credited greed as the driving force behind the progress of Western civilization. The unsung hero of free enterprise. Greed had been around a long time; many souls less vulnerable than Grace Shipley had succumbed to its seductiveness.

Was Grace responsible for the deaths of Jimmy Pigeon, Walter Richman, and Jack Canty? Yes, partly.

Could she have prevented their deaths? Perhaps.

Could anything be done to change these events? Nothing.

Could I judge her and condemn her?

I didn't feel qualified.

Sally had said to me once, I can't recall the circumstance, that there was no mystery to life; it just happened. Whatever was going to happen with Grace's life, I decided that I would be no part of it.

"Grace."

"Yes?" She sat on the bed, staring at the floor.

"Grace, look at me."

She looked up into my eyes.

"It's all over, Grace. I'll keep you out of it."

"I wondered, especially after Frank killed Jimmy, why he hadn't just killed me in the first place, before he signed me on for half the score. And I could only think of one reason, and this is the really sick part in all of this. Frank seriously believed that after we collected the money we would stay together and live happily ever after."

"Consider yourself lucky that he was still in love with you."

I considered myself very lucky that I wasn't still in love with her.

"I was planning to kill Frank. When I got to the island."

"Grace, you can leave now," I said.

"Leave?"

"Yes, please."

"Where do I go?"

"I can't help you."

She didn't have to tell me that she understood.

She rose slowly from the bed, straightened her dress, moved to the door, and opened it. She hesitated for a split second and walked out.

I sat, my eyes closed, my mind blank.

An hour had gone by unnoticed when the telephone rang.

Sonny.

"Isla Margarita, Venezuela. I would have

326

called you from the air, but there was no phone; the plane was so small I'm surprised it had a cockpit."

"Is it done?"

"Mission accomplished. I stopped Slater as he was fumbling with his room key. You would have loved it, Jake. I put a Coca-Cola bottleneck in his back and said, 'Move and I'll shoot.' He turned to jelly. When we got inside the room I knocked him out cold with the pop bottle. Don't worry, he'll live, but he's going to have a whopping headache. Villa Cabo Blanco. Room Six-eleven. I took the money and put it in a safe-deposit box at the nearest bank."

Sonny read off the pertinent information.

"Great job, Sonny."

"I took Slater's passport, all of his other identification, and most of his pocket cash. I left him a few bucks for aspirin. He's going to be stuck there for a while. I have to run; there's a flight out of here in less than an hour."

"OK, thanks. I'll speak with you when you get back."

I called Detective Boyle in Los Angeles.

"Ray, there's twenty million dollars in two banks down in the Caribbean. I'll give you the details and you can pass them on to Richman International or the insurance company or whatever."

"That's a lot of bread, Jake," he said, after taking down the information. "Weren't you just a little tempted?"

"What would I do with twenty million bucks, Ray? If it weren't for my addictions to Dickel, Camels, and Mylanta I wouldn't know how to spend the few hundred I already have."

"Where's Slater?"

"He got away."

"Was he in it alone?"

"As far as I know."

"OK, Jake, so long."

I was pretty sure that Boyle didn't believe me, but Ray had known for a long time what I had only learned in the past few days: trying to discover what's not ready to be discovered is like trying to catch water in a net.

I had one more phone call to make and then I could get out of that godforsaken hotel room.

"Carlucci's Restaurant, Tony speaking."

"Room Six-eleven. Villa Cabo Blanco. Isla Margarita, Venezuela," I said.

"Drop by for dinner sometime, Diamond. I'm buying."

"I'll think about it," I said, and hung up the phone.

I picked up the carton of cigarettes and left the room.

THIRTY-TWO

It's amazing how quickly things can get right back to normal.

I had picked up a few new clients during the following week; the cases were far from unusual or challenging.

I had spoken briefly with Hannah Sims. She called asking if I knew where Grace had gone. I didn't. Hannah said that Grace had disappeared. Grace had the vanishing act down pat.

"Grace is a survivor, Hannah," I said.

It was the best I could do.

A check for twenty thousand dollars had come to the office from Dick Spencer, written out to Tina Bella Pazzo. Tina had let Darlene know where to send the money when it arrived. I sent fifteen thousand down to Tina, somewhere in Mexico. I would give the five grand that remained back to Joey for the grubstake he'd given Tina when she left.

I sent the thousand down to Myron Coolidge that Joey had promised him, from what I had left of Carlucci's cash. The kid had earned it.

After expenses for Darlene and Sonny's island adventure I still had enough money left over to buy a new coffee machine for the office and a few neckties.

I felt I was finally ready for the ties.

The twenty million had been collected from the banks in Cayman and Venezuela and returned to Richman International. I received a thank-you card from the acting CEO.

As far as Frank Slater was concerned, he was nowhere to be found. And he never would be.

I was sitting at home on a Saturday evening when Joey Russo called.

"Jake, I just heard from Tony Carlucci. He'd like to buy you dinner. Thank you properly for giving him Frank Slater. I told him that I didn't think you'd be interested."

"You said that I wasn't interested?"

"Well, maybe I said you weren't available. In any case, I thought I'd pass Tony's appreciation on."

"What happened to Slater?"

"You don't want to know."

"Maybe I'll take Tony up on his dinner invite. There's some unfinished business he might be able to help with if he's as appreciative as he says he is."

"What's on your mind?"

"Something I've been thinking about for the past few days. If you'll join me, I can run it by you on our way over to Carlucci's."

"I don't know, Jake. Angela is cooking up a storm over here."

"Joey, I could really use your help on this."

"I thought I'd never hear you say it, Jake. I'll pick you up in an hour."

The white-haired dinner-jacketed waiters brought more, more, and then more food for nearly two hours. There wasn't one waiter at Carlucci's who looked to be less than sixty years old; I imagined that every one of them had worked the room for forty years. The Chianti was the seventy-five-dollar-a-bottle variety. Mama Carlucci kept coming up to the table to make sure that we were all chewing. Joey had assured me that there would be no discussion of business until the final dinner plate was removed from the table, until coffee, anisette, and dessert were in place. The coffee was black and strong, the liqueur was imported, and the pastry was homemade.

"So," said Carlucci, getting right down to

business, "Joey tells me you have something to ask, Jake. Mind if I call you Jake?"

"Not at all, Mr. Carlucci," I said.

"I appreciate your honoring the arrangement I had with Jimmy Pigeon," he said, "but remember that I was told there would be no strings attached."

"I remember."

"On top of that, I have an idea that you had your own reasons for dealing with Slater's punishment the way you did. It's none of my business."

He waited a moment, decided I had nothing to say, and went on.

"That being said, I'll do what I can. Of course, as I'm sure Joey told you, it will have to be rubber-stamped by my brother John."

Carlucci was taking the meeting very seriously. I was hoping it was a good sign.

"I understand," I said.

"Good. So what can I do for you?"

"I just wanted your advice, Mr. Carlucci," I said, "your opinion."

"Go ahead."

"A man tries to save a friend. In doing so he makes a personal sacrifice. He puts loyalty before personal preference, personal gain, and personal safety."

"Commendable," said Carlucci.

"His commendable action costs him his

life; the friend he tried to save also loses his life; the man responsible goes unpunished."

"Jake, do me a favor: skip the hypothetical and tell me what you want."

I thought I caught Joey Russo suppressing a smile.

"You made a deal with Jimmy Pigeon. If he gave you Slater, you would take care of a debt to Al Pazzo. It wasn't Jimmy's debt; he was trying to rescue his friend Harry Harding. Al Pazzo didn't kill Jimmy, but the deal Jimmy made with you may have. And Pazzo did kill Harding, who had a wife and a teenage daughter. I'd like to see Pazzo pay."

"I can't hit Al Pazzo."

"That's not what I had in mind," I said.

And then I explained to Tony Carlucci what he could do for me.

Carlucci allowed me to listen in on his office phone; he made the call from the telephone at the bar.

"Let me speak with Mr. Pazzo," he said. "This is Tony Carlucci."

"Tony, how are you?"

"Good, Al. Listen, you know a PI named Diamond?"

"Yeah. What about him?" Pazzo asked.

"Diamond was just in here, putting a good dent into one of my bourbon bottles. It loosened his tongue. He said that Joey Russo is leaning hard on him; Diamond owes on some ill-advised basketball wagers. Diamond said he was coming down to LA to get the money he needs to pay off Russo. From you."

"How does he plan to do that?"

"Diamond claims that you left Harry Harding alive long enough to name you. He thinks that his silence might be worth a few bucks to you."

"He can't touch me. There's no evidence; it's his word against mine."

"Granted, but put his story together with Evelyn Harding's testimony that you were threatening Harding and Bobo Bigelow's testimony that you knew where Harding was holed up, well, it could cause some unnecessary heat. I just thought that you might want to know."

"Diamond is a bug; he doesn't worry me. But I appreciate it, Tony," Pazzo said.

"No problem. Take it easy, Al; good luck."

The line went dead.

I wondered if it would be enough to be able to tell Evelyn Harding that I'd tried.

That's if I would be able to talk at all after Pazzo was through with me.

It was a gamble.

I lost.

The phone rang.

"Tony."

"Al? What's up?"

"While Diamond was flapping his tongue, did he happen to mention my wife?"

"No."

"Is Diamond still around?"

"No, he left for the airport to catch his flight down there. And not a minute too soon. Joey Russo just walked in looking for him."

"Can I speak with Russo?"

"Sure, hold on."

"Al."

"Joey, how much is Diamond into you for?"

"That's between Diamond and me, Al," said Joey. "You know that."

"Take it easy. I thought I could help you out is all."

Joey paused just long enough.

"About ten grand, Al."

"How about I take care of it, and throw in a little bonus, let's say five more?"

"What's the catch?"

"Tony C. says that Diamond is trying to lay a murder rap on me, this guy Harding. I mean the fucking guy is delusional, but I could do without the attention. And I'm not going to let a loser like Diamond blackmail me; it's not good for my image. I'd like to shut Diamond up, but I don't want you to get stiffed for what he owes you."

"That's good of you, Al."

"Common courtesy, Joey," Al said.

It was going just as Joey Russo had said it would, almost word for word.

"Listen, Al," Joey said after a beat. "I have an idea how you can take care of Diamond and take the Harding murder off the books at the same time."

"Oh?"

"There's a lieutenant down there: Ray Boyle."

"Yeah, I know him," said Pazzo.

"Boyle doesn't like open homicide cases; it's against his religion or something. He's going to keep the pressure on. At first he liked Diamond for the Harding murder; Boyle was thinking that Diamond killed Harding as payback for Jimmy Pigeon. Boyle even has Diamond's prints at the scene, but no murder weapon."

"OK."

"Diamond is on his way down there; he's headed for his cousin's place in Westwood somewhere," Joey said.

"I know the place," Pazzo said.

"I don't care what happens to Diamond, as long as I get my cash. The guy is a

336

menace. Next thing you know he'll be threatening me."

Joey was convincing; it sent a shiver down my spine.

"But if Boyle found the gun that killed Harry Harding with Diamond," Joey said, "it could solve Boyle's problem and yours. It's just a thought, Al. Makes more sense than icing Diamond and getting Boyle all stirred up over another open homicide."

"How would the gun that killed Harding wind up with Diamond?" asked Pazzo.

"I have no idea, Al. Diamond gets into LA in a few hours. Maybe the piece is already there. I gotta run, Al. Good luck."

Joey hung up the bar phone.

I hung up the office phone and called Ray Boyle. Then I went out to the bar. Tony Carlucci was gone.

Joey ushered me out of the restaurant and into his car.

"Well?" I said, as Joey started for my place on Fillmore Street.

"Call Evelyn Harding. Let her know you tried at least," Joey said.

THIRTY-THREE

Ray Boyle called me the next morning. Sunday.

They had picked up Al Pazzo's driver going into my cousin Bobby's place. He was carrying the gun that killed Harry Harding. He quickly gave Pazzo up.

"The guy told us where we could dig up a few more bodies," said Ray. "We have Pazzo locked up without bail. He's not going to see the street again for a long time."

"Think he'll send someone after me?"

"I think I convinced him that I was after you to begin with, that we had the place staked out waiting for you to show. With any luck, Pazzo will appreciate the irony and concentrate more on his own immediate situation."

"Thanks, Ray," I said.

"Jake."

"Yeah, Ray."

"I got a strange call just after Frank Slater

disappeared. A woman, she wouldn't identify herself."

"Oh?"

"She said that Frank Slater definitely
killed Jimmy Pigeon. She said that she was
there when it happened. I'll look into it,"
Boyle said.

And he rang off.

Grace had come with Slater that night to
talk with Jimmy.

It explained how Slater had gotten close
enough to put a bullet from Harry Harding's gun into Jimmy's chest.

It explained the hell that Grace said she
would have to inhabit, jail time or none.

I kept busy during the week working a few
cases.

I tried reaching Vinnie a few times, but he
seemed to be avoiding me.

Come to think of it, and not to sound
paranoid, it felt like everyone had been
avoiding me for days. Angela Russo told me
that Joey was out of town every time I called.
Sonny always seemed to be off with him.
The guys I played poker with on Thursday
nights called off the game without good
reason. I left a few messages on Sally's machine and hadn't heard back from her. I'd
called Lincoln French, to thank him again
for his help, but always got his answering

service. Darlene had made herself scarce since returning from the island, said she needed a few days off, her boyfriend was in town, this and that.

Jesus, even my mother seemed to be dodging me.

I called Mom to invite myself to dinner on the upcoming Saturday and she said she was busy.

Could we make it sometime next week?

I found Darlene at work when I came in on Friday. She told me she had a load of catching up to do, so I shouldn't bother her at all. I went into my office and sat at my desk twiddling my thumbs.

At around noon Darlene buzzed to say I had a call.

"Jake."

"Sam?"

"I can't talk long; there's a line of inmates behind me who gave up on patience a long time ago. I just wanted to wish you a Happy Birthday."

"Thanks, Sam. I really appreciate the thought." I was touched that Sam had remembered, and had put himself through the turmoil of lining up to make a prison phone call.

"I have to run, Jake," he said after a very short dialogue.

"I'll be down to see you soon, Sam. Next week, in fact; count on it." And I would.

I walked out into the reception area and stood stupidly at Darlene's desk.

"What?" she said, looking up at me with annoyance.

"That was Sam Chambers calling to wish me a Happy Birthday."

"That was sweet of him. Don't expect another present from me, Jake; I gave you your shirt already," she said. "I thought your birthday was tomorrow."

"Yeah, it is," I said, and went back to my room.

I lasted there for another two or three minutes and couldn't stand it any longer. I told Darlene, if she cared, that I was heading out for lunch.

"Can I bring you anything?" I asked.

"No thanks," she said; then she stopped what she was doing and looked up at me. "Listen, Jake, why don't you take the rest of the day off? There's nothing going on here; it's almost the weekend anyway. I'm not staying long myself. Go catch a movie or something; you look like you don't know what to do with yourself."

"Maybe I will. Have a good weekend."

"You do the same," she said. "I'll see you back here on Monday."

I left the office and walked down to Columbus Avenue.

What the hell. What did I have to be so depressed about? So I was turning forty years old the next day. What was that, the end of the world or something? What was the big deal? So my mother was busy tomorrow night. When was the last time I changed my plans for *her* birthday?

I could entertain myself, treat myself. Business wasn't bad, the rent was paid on my office and apartment, and I still had pocket cash.

I'd start with lunch at Little Mike's. The works.

Maybe I *would* catch a movie. I hadn't seen one in at least six months.

For dinner I'd buy myself the biggest porterhouse in San Francisco and the most expensive bottle of Cabernet.

As for the next day, as for my fortieth birthday.

Well, I'd never been one for planning too far ahead.

THIRTY-FOUR

When I woke up Saturday morning I wasn't feeling too bad. Considering. I had thrown quite the bash for myself, from the middle of the day before through late into the night.

Wisely I had imbibed only the finest wine.

Truth be told, I felt much better than just OK, inasmuch as I had been knocking around the planet since 1960.

I jumped in and out of the shower and headed into the kitchen to try out the new coffeemaker. When I picked one up for the office I decided to buy another for the ranch while I was at it. The result was very good. I'm sure the fact that the coffee came from Hawaii and was priced at $17.99 a pound didn't hurt.

I was enjoying the morning, reading the *Examiner.* The Giants were making a run at the first-place Arizona Diamondbacks. I was doing the continental thing with a sourdough baguette and seedless raspberry jam.

I was on my third cup of coffee with not a serious thought in my head when the phone rang.

"Jake?"

"Sally?"

"How are you?"

"Not too bad."

"I just got back into town. I wanted to know if things worked out all right. You had me worried there for a minute."

"You know me, Sal. I land on my feet."

I said it, but that shouldn't imply that I knew what it was supposed to mean.

"I was wondering," she said.

"Oh?"

"I thought that if you didn't have anything special planned you might want to come over for dinner tonight."

Now I might have felt embarrassed to admit that I had nothing going for me on a Saturday night, but look at it this way: it was better than having to remind Sally that it was my birthday and I had nothing special planned.

So why not?

"That sounds great, Sally; what time?"

"How about eight?"

"I'll be there. I'll bring some wine."

How about that?

I spent the rest of the morning feeling

anxious about dinner with Sally. God knows why. I suddenly realized that I'd probably find Dick Spencer there with us, sucking his food through a straw. There was a thought to bring me right back to earth. At least it inspired me to stop agonizing about it, which in turn helped get me through the day and over to the wine shop and to her door at the house in the Presidio.

I took a deep breath and rang the doorbell.

When she opened the door I held out the wine bottle and grinned like an idiot.

"Come in," she said.

"What are you planning to do with the wine, Jake?" It was Joey Russo's unmistakable voice. "We have twelve bottles of Dickel here that need immediate attention."

I turned toward Joey as he was pulling a bottle out of the cardboard case.

Standing beside him was Sonny, with his wife, Joey's daughter, Connie. And Angela Russo, holding onto Joey's arm like a cheerleader claiming her hero.

"Happy Birthday, Jake," they all said at once.

And there were other voices also.

I looked around the room in astonishment.

"Hey, old man," said Vinnie Strings, "the

odds down at the Finnish Line were that you'd never make it to forty."

"Did you lean in my favor, Vin?"

"You bet, Jake. I cleaned up."

Lincoln French and his wife were there. The fact that Jenny came meant a lot to me.

The jokers I played poker with were all there.

"Deal 'em, Jake!" someone shouted, and they all broke out laughing.

Darlene was there, of course, with her football player.

"Here, Jake. Happy Birthday," she said, handing me a baseball signed by Willie Mays. "Lughead has connections in the sports world if nothing else."

My cousin Bobby Sanders the actor, just back from the shoot in Mexico, appeared to shake my hand. His mother, Aunt Rosalie, was there, with her new boyfriend. The man wasn't quite a hundred twenty years old, maybe only seventy-five.

And then I spotted my mother, on the sidelines waiting to be spotted.

"It was so difficult to say no to you when you called, Son, to ask if you could come for dinner. I've felt terrible for days."

"Thanks for the surprise, Mom," I said. "Speaking of food, something smells great. You didn't come over here to cook, did you?"

"Oh, no. The food was prepared by a lovely woman who delivered it fresh less than twenty minutes ago. Mr. Russo called her Mama Carlucci."

"Telephone, Jake!" I heard Darlene call out.

"Hello," I said into the receiver.

"Happy Birthday, Jake."

"Tina?"

"I can't stay on the line; I just wanted to thank you for everything. I'm doing fine."

After speaking with Tina I heard a familiar voice and turned to find Myron Coolidge, boy wonder, standing beside me.

"Happy Birthday, Mr. Diamond," he said.

"Thanks for coming, kid; ever try George Dickel?"

"Who's that?"

"Follow me," I said.

I'd never been to a surprise party in my life where I believed that the victim was really surprised.

Until that night.

Sally looked fantastic, and Dick Spencer was conspicuously absent.

"How is Richard doing?" I asked her when I had a chance to get her alone for a moment.

"Dick and I had a little falling-out," she said.

There was a lot I felt like saying, but I decided it could wait. Maybe I would call her during the week. I was almost about to say something inane, just to say something, when Darlene bounced up to us and held out an envelope.

"What's this?" I asked.

"It came to the office yesterday. Sorry I opened it; I thought it was a bill."

"Cheap bastards only gave you one percent," said Joey, coming up to join us.

I took the check out of the envelope. It was a finder's reward from the insurance company that covered Richman International. It was written out to me in the amount of $200,000.

"That should keep you in Mylanta for a while," Darlene laughed.

Actually, I knew exactly what I would do with the money. Fifty grand would go to Darlene and another fifty to Sonny, for their trip to the island.

I would put fifty aside for Sam Chambers, for when he got out of the Men's Colony, to get him started in good shape.

For a moment I thought about giving the rest to Vinnie, but I decided to keep it myself so I'd have cash for all the times he was going to hit me up for a loan that he would never pay back.

Later in the evening I felt George Dickel doing a little dance in my head. I felt I could use some fresh air and a cigarette. I'm a die-hard believer that the two aren't mutually exclusive.

I walked through the kitchen and out the back door into the small yard behind the house. I sat down in the cedar armchair and lit a Camel. I had spent many evenings in that chair during the time I lived with Sally, listening to the noise of the city and gazing at the Golden Gate Bridge.

I realized that I loved San Francisco, maybe as much as Jimmy Pigeon had loved Los Angeles. I understood that even though Jimmy and I had drifted apart, we were both where we wanted and needed to be.

I thought that Charles Dickens could re-late.

I thought about the people inside the house. What really amazed me was not so much the surprise of finding them all there as the fact that they had all made the effort.

They were all there to celebrate with a sap who had made a habit of pushing them away.

I promised myself that I wouldn't forget their clemency.

The night could hardly have been better, although it would have been terrific to see

Jimmy Pigeon there. I remembered something Jimmy said to me the last time I'd spoken with him.

"It's not what you know *or* who you know," he said. "It's how far you are willing to go to know better."

Sitting there on my fortieth birthday, watching the headlights of the cars crossing the Golden Gate, I finally got it.

"How are you doing, Jake?"

I turned from the bridge to see Joey Russo heading for me with a bottle of bourbon in one hand and two glasses filled with ice in the other.

"Good, Joey," I said. "Real good."

He filled the two glasses and handed one to me.

"So," I asked, "how's Carmella?"

"Beautiful," Joey said, "unbelievable."

Joey and I talked about his granddaughter.

When the ice was gone we went back to the party.